TWISTED

TWISTED

BONDAGE WITH AN EDGE

EDITED BY
ALISON TYLER

CLEiS
PRESS

Published in the United States by Cleis Press, Inc., 2246 Sixth Street, Berkeley, California 94710.

Printed in the United States.
Cover design: Scott Idleman/Blink
Cover photograph: Willie B. Thomas/Getty Images
Text design: Frank Wiedemann

First Edition.
10 9 8 7 6 5 4 3 2 1

Trade paper ISBN: 978-1-62778-008-7
E-book ISBN: 978-1-62778-021-6

Contents

INTRODUCTION: GIMME A KINK!

By now you know that I'm on a search, a quest, a journey into the unknown. Oh, wait. That's not right. I *do* know bondage. I know it like the back of my bound hands. After editing *Best Bondage Erotica* (volumes 1 and 2), *Hurts So Good*, *Love at First Sting*, *B Is for Bondage*, *Pleasure Bound* and a slew of others, I definitely am well-acquainted with the words and world of the BDSM trade. But that doesn't mean I've had enough. I can't get enough. There's *never* enough.

I've been a bondage fanatic since I first understood that the word *obey* could be used in a bedroom. That on my knees on a hardwood floor could be sexier than sprawled in a bed of silken, leopard-print sheets. That a velvet blindfold over my eyes or cold steel cuffs on my wrists could make my heart pitter-patter faster than a bouquet of scarlet roses or a glittery piece of jewelry.

And that's how the authors in *Twisted* feel, as well. These are the stories that delve deep down into what bondage means, stories that will make you perk up and take notice. Or bind you down and make you behave.

Like this snippet from Kristina Lloyd's transcendent "Dry Spell":

I hadn't realized what a sadist my new boyfriend was until I'd granted him control of my orgasms. I hadn't realized, either, what a thrill I'd get from doing as I was told, from obeying Ray's orders even when he wasn't there.

See? There's that word *obey*.

And again, in Veronica Wilde's dreamy "Wilderness Test":

"I knew you were a disobedient counselor, but I had no idea you'd need this much discipline. You are going to be retrained, starting now. Lesson one: obey your senior counselor."

Suddenly, her tied wrists were rising over her head. Dax was tying her to something overhead, probably a tree branch.

I love when the Doms talk like that. You can hear the timbre of his voice, can't you? You can close your eyes and fall into the story.

N. T. Morley's "The Saturday Pet" takes things to a different level:

Tera was trained and usually obedient. Sometimes she did not obey her owner—and then she was punished.

How else could a pet be defined?

After all these years, and all these collections, I'm filled to brimming with grateful glee each time I discover a new gem. I want the tools to be the same—those treasured, utilitarian devices that make me sit up straighter, make me pay attention. But I want the tales to be brand-new. Sparkling, like a chrome collar on a black piece of leather.

This collection fulfills my needs—my desperate cravings—with stellar, ethereal, beautiful writing, and kink at the core.

XXX,
Alison

TIE ME UP

Andrea Dale

T ie me up. Please.

I know you like it when I beg.

Tie me up. It's the only way I can feel free, only way I can let go. Shiny clanking handcuffs, smooth ropes, silk scarves, red leather fur-lined restraints, your red-dotted Burberry tie.

I want it. I need it. I crave it.

And then there's you. You need it, too, don't you? You need to see me relax into my bonds, accept the place you've let me escape to.

When my eyes close for the blindfold, you brush a soft kiss on my lips and whisper, "I love you."

FOUNDATION
STONE

Jax Baynard

The house was not yet a house, though it had a roof and four walls which suggested it might one day become one. The inside was cool and dim, light coming from the paneless windows open to the dusky sky. Julia prowled, her running shoes quiet on the subfloors. The rough framing formed skeletal hands between the rooms. Kitchen, laundry room, guest bath, the hall with its high ceiling already in shadow. She ran lightly up the stairs of Carrara marble, starkly formal against the plywood, impervious to weather and time. She moved soundlessly through the upstairs rooms, master bedroom and bath—the latter alone the size of her living room—thinking of the lives that would be lived here. They would have money, whoever these people were. More marble in the bathroom, this time of a soft pink variety, with thready gray veining, as if a burly man from one of the Italian quarrying families had shown up, installed his marble on his own time and departed, leaving behind him a trail of sawdust, ruined schedules, change orders and coffee stains.

She found a back staircase off one of the smaller bedrooms and emerged in the great room. All the houses in the Hollywood Hills had one, to take advantage of the view, ostensibly, but also to say without words: *This is how much money I have. You?* Julia had no money to speak of. She had brown hair and green eyes and if she had a great body it was because she took it running come rain (never very likely) or shine for an hour and a half most days. She was not a model or an actress. She was not working on a screenplay. She was not a waitress, aspiring to be a model or an actress. She lived, for nominal rent, in the guesthouse of a friend of her Aunt Gwyne's and she worked at the observatory. She was single, though she dated enough to know the myth about men always wanting sex was a myth. She was hard pressed to find one who wanted it once a week, much less once a day.

"Trespassing?" someone said.

Technically, she wasn't. There were no doors, just openings where they would be, eventually, with locks connected to an expensive security system. "Yes," she said. It was him. She thought of him as the Builder; he was probably the architect or the site manager. She had walked past for five months, from when the house was nothing but a gouge in the hillside. She did not always see him. Occasionally, he lifted a hand in greeting and she waved back. They had never spoken and she had never been this close to him. "Nice marble," she said.

"Not quite your speed?" he asked, coming into the room.

Julia shrugged. "Is the house a home yet?"

He glanced at her, then pondered, in the gathering twilight, what was left of the view. Pinpricks of light were beginning to show through the haze. "The little people down on the flats," she had a heard a visitor at the observatory call them.

"It has an owner, if that's what you're asking. I don't know if that will make it a home." He shrugged in turn.

He was good looking, this man, Julia thought. A genetic accident, her mother would have said. Her mother was a scientist. She thought in molecules and double twists of DNA. It was her way of saying *Pretty is as pretty does.* It's what's inside the person that counts. Julia thought of the clothes she had left, the jewels, the walk-in closet the size of her entire house, the marriage she had walked out of, and felt the great burden of weariness she carried with her, always. It took time to know a person; years, in fact. This man might have hidden depths, glittering at the bottom of the ocean like treasure. He might be half a man. She had no way of knowing.

"My name is Graham," he said. He held out his hand. Julia looked at it like an offering made in a country where one is unfamiliar with the customs, but it did not waver. She put her hand in his. It was not bad to be touching him.

"Julia," she said. She stared at him in what little light was left. Dark hair, light eyes, tanned skin. A bump in his otherwise aquiline nose. Wide shoulders, a solid body, as if he, too, spent time somewhere other than standing around a construction site all day. She realized she liked having her hand in his.

"Would you like a cup of coffee?" he asked, and Julia had a brief memory, a flicker in celluloid, of a coffeepot sitting on the granite countertop in the kitchen.

"I'd rather have bourbon," she said.

He had not let go of her hand. It was nearly dark, but a glow coming from behind him said the house was electrified and there was a light on somewhere. "That could be arranged," he said. He pulled her a step closer. "Do you know what a foundation stone is?"

She shook her head, wanting to know what he smelled like. It was important, what men smelled like. It was what the sheets would smell like the next morning.

"Before there was concrete"—his hand continued to hold hers; the other began to learn the shape of her forearm from wrist to elbow—"foundations were built of stone. Builders were usually the owners of the houses and it was the custom in that country to lay a foundation stone, sometimes near the hearth, sometimes at the north corner of the house, marked with the date and name of the family. This was known"—he was touching her bicep, her shoulder, trailing his fingers across her exposed collarbones, his touch overtly sexual now—"as the first memory of the house." Julia did not move away and that was answer enough. "I'm going to kiss you," he said, giving her time to object. She didn't move. It was her neck he kissed. And sucked. And licked. "I'll keep doing this until you touch me," he murmured, as if she had forgotten an item of protocol.

Julia lifted her hands, till now hanging by her sides like so much flotsam. She put them on his back, pulling up the tails of his shirt to absorb the warmth of his skin. "Here?" she asked. "Now?" She had learned to be direct. It saved time.

He stopped what he was doing to look at her. He pulled the tie from her hair and smoothed the tangles with his fingers. "What do you need?" he said.

"I want to feel something other than disgust," Julia said. She could feel the pounding of her own heart, the liquid rush between her legs, the prickling of sweat across her chest.

Graham kissed her again, not on the mouth. "I want to tie you up," he said, "and fuck you." Her eyes widened only slightly. He could be direct, too. "Will you run?" he said. He lifted his hands, making it easy for her to go.

"I don't think so," she answered.

He walked away. "On this," he said.

"Painful," Julia replied. The table he indicated was a table saw. The blade was twelve inches across and curved teeth curled around the rim like waves in a Hokusai print of the sea. He flipped a lever and the blade sank out of sight. He picked up the cord and held it. Julia walked to where he stood. Closer, she could see the dark flush staining his cheekbones, evidence that he was not as calm as he seemed. This was not a date. She did not have to play by those rules. This was not an assignation, something her ex-husband was very much in favor of. She did not know what this was. The man next to her had not moved except to gauge her height and make another adjustment to the table and now he waited, not speaking. A fall, Julia decided. A jump from a precipice. But the ground was a long way off.

She expected him to taunt her. *Scared? Can't make up your mind? Run away, little girl.* He touched her again, running a calloused fingertip from the hollow of her throat to her nipple, surprisingly gentle. The nipple pebbled anyway, making her shudder. She had been married on her twenty-first birthday and she was thirty-two. The number of decisions she made every day was appalling. She sometimes tried to avoid making any, but then there were more the next day, piled up on her doormat like unopened mail. To be tied down? To have someone else make the decisions, even for half an hour? She was delirious from the thought. "On or off?" She gestured to her top.

"Like this." He pulled it up until her breasts were exposed, but left it on. He bent and sucked her nipples until her legs gave out, then he bent her over the saw. He tied one hand with the cord, looping it over her wrist several times and knotting it to the leg. The other hand he tied with duct tape. She felt the adhesive on the fine hairs of her wrist. He tugged, and she felt an answering throb in her pussy. He spread her legs, putting her feet where he wanted them. He peeled down her running tights, leaving the material bunched below her hips. Everything was hard—the table, the floor, the walls, the man behind her, her memories (how do you say you love someone for ten years and wake up one day and not like what you see?)—except her flesh, pale and yielding. His breathing roughened. "Every day I thought of this," he said, opening her with his hands. "Every time I saw your ass twitch by, I imagined this."

She was wet already, drenched. "I thought you were busy," Julia said.

"Not that busy," he countered.

If she turned her head she could find the view, but she didn't want it. She wanted the dark and the waiting; and the feeling, when it came, pulled an inhuman sound from her throat.

"Go ahead," he told her. "There's no one to hear." He pushed into her with one hard, sure thrust. It bore no resemblance to the inept fumblings of men who needed permission to start and praise when it was over. The table threatened to roll with the force of his thrusts and he flipped a switch to stop it. The wheels locked in place. Julia turned her face against the cold metal, her nipples rubbing on the fine corrugations of the surface. Her hands strained against the bonds; her right had enough room to twist and hold the table leg. Her left, held fast in the tape, flexed and fisted on air. It went on for a long time. He was strong and big and he pushed her through the first heady spasms of desire. He felt the instant her body surrendered to the hard work of fucking; he dragged her from there to a place where, even as she tensed to take him, again and again, her body went liquid and hot and she couldn't control her limbs so he did it for her.

By the time he pushed her to her toes and slid a hand beneath her belly, slippery with sweat, she had forgotten about her clit. There was only the friction of his cock pounding into her body, and that was all she wanted, but he made her remember her clit. It was too much. She howled against it, but he made her feel that, too. She came. She came and felt the heat of her blood everywhere in her body, but mostly where he was touching her.

He untied the cord. He got a knife and cut through the tape, pulling it away from her skin without mercy. He pulled her top down and her tights up and, since standing on her own legs proved to be unsuccessful, he carried her into the kitchen. He set her down on the counter where she remained upright, barely. He fetched the bourbon, good Kentucky bourbon. It was his house. The first thing he had done when there were counters and cabinets was to put a coffee pot on the counter and bourbon in the cabinet.

She came back into herself, enough to watch him with curious eyes. The first sip he took in his own mouth and with a hand on the nape of her neck, let it trickle into hers. That was the first time he kissed her. They drank the bourbon slowly. They watched the headlights making rivers through the stars, fixed and burning, below them.

LOVE TO HATE

Molly Moore

The cuffs are tight on my wrists and ankles, and when I pull on them I can hear the distinctive sound of chains. The room is silent but for that, and I lie there behind the dark of the blindfold playing with my own bonds. Pulling and twisting, making them talk to me. Their voice fits perfectly into my darkness, and despite knowing I'm here in this room, my mind slips to dungeons, guards and an evil captivity.

I'm happy here in this place, naked, vulnerable and blind. I wait for you, knowing you will come for me. For now my mind draws pictures for me, of who you are, and why you have me here like this. I know I should be scared of the unknown and ashamed of my nakedness, but then I have never been very good at what I should be; why should chains and darkness and an electric fear change that now?

My body aches. I am glad of the moment's respite from your abuse and yet I miss you already. My playful toying with the chains soon turns to a restful impatience. I hate waiting, I hate being left. I hate not knowing. I hate being played with. I live for this hate and the way you make me face my darkness. I love my hate. It is a passion.

The sound of the whip still rings. My body twitches at the memory of the split ends trailing their evil kisses across my breasts leaving bright red welts in their wake. I moan at the memory, and I crave more. I know the heat between my thighs betrays my love of the hate.

You're silent in your approach, and I'm so lost in my own body and mind that it's not until I feel the bed shift under your weight that I know you're back. Without a thought of the consequences words of admonishment spit from my mouth....

"Don't leave me like this. Just do what you want with—"

The rest is muffled by your hand, words of venom and anger lost into your grip and silenced completely by your soft gentle, "Shhhh." My tongue flicks out, tasting your palm; tentative at first, then with increasing greed until I am suckling on the soft flesh at the base of your thumb. I feast on you, my mouth consuming anything that you're willing to give.

When you move your hand away, my mouth feels desolately empty, pleading noises fill the back of my throat and like a little bird in the nest, or a hungry baby at the breast, my mouth searches anxiously for you.

I hate you even more. You're playing with me, like a cat plays with a wounded mouse until it's so broken all it can do is give itself up to the monster that has captured it. The hate charges through my body, sending pulses of electric desire into my cunt, making me throb with agonizing need.

Your fingers curl into my hair, twisting it round until you have a firm grasp. Your cock is hard and hot against my lips, and I willingly open my mouth. I don't care who you are anymore. I just want you to fill me up and consume what is left of my rage. Your grip tightens in my hair as you use my mouth to pleasure yourself, gliding your cock in and out, slowly but firmly, each time a little bit deeper than the time before. I know I'm dribbling, I can feel it running down my cheek and pooling beside my face. My fingers tingle with the need to reach between my thighs and rub at my throbbing clit. You ignore my choking sobs. Or at least that is how it feels to me, but then I can't see you. I can't see the delicious grin that plays across your lips as you watch me struggle against my bonds. I can't see you clenching your teeth as you fight to control the urge to come in my mouth, and I can't see your other hand holding something small and round reaching between my legs.

The cold against the heat of my thighs makes me moan against your cock, and then the vibrations start. On my thigh, then down into the line of my groin making my hips dance as I try to guide your hand into my cunt. My thrashing is futile, my bonds are too tight to allow me that pleasure and as you roll the powerful vibrator all around the edge of my throbbing pussy, I growl with a deep guttural noise of rage and lust.

You play on, ignoring my cries, filling my mouth with slow purposeful strokes, making my jaw ache and my lips sting. Between my thighs you tease and torture, letting the vibe glide over my clit, causing my hips to buck and tremble before you move away. Each pass brings me closer toward release and yet each pass builds the painful ache within. My mouth and cunt slowly blend together. As one is plundered and used by you the other pulses and twitches in a jealous desperation.

Anger boils through my veins at my body's traitorous lust. Whoever you are, you have stolen my lust and used it against me. Your come is hot and thick inside my mouth. It coats my tongue and runs down my lips, but I barely notice it as you cruelly press the vibe against my clit, cupping your hand over my cunt and holding me firmly beneath you. Now my orgasm tears through my body. My legs thrash and my back arches as my cunt releases its juices. Behind the blindfold, tears gather and roll down my cheeks.

Stripping the blindfold from my face you brush my tears aside, and at last I can see you.

"Have I mentioned how much I hate you?" I grumble.

"Often," you laughingly reply, "but I don't believe a word of it."

DRY SPELL

Kristina Lloyd

I realized my orgasms were controlling the weather when, for the umpteenth time, rain came crashing down as I climaxed. The curtains billowed in the sudden chill, the windows rattled as rain hammered at the glass and a car alarm honked in the street. Coincidence, you might say, but this had happened too often to be dismissed as a fluke.

On the first occasion, Ray had lifted his head from between my thighs and joked, "How do you do that?" I'd laughed lazily, thinking little of it. Half-drugged with postorgasmic bliss, I'd watched water sluice down the window in rolling, silvery screens, and pour from the ledge above, shimmering and swaying like a row of dancing icicles. I'd felt as if my peak were being applauded, my wetness honored with a show of wetness from the skies.

But when it continued to happen, we realized we had a problem. Ray and I had been having phenomenal amounts of sex in the months we'd been dating. During that time, the

United Kingdom had experienced one of the worst summers on record. The Met Office issued regular severe weather warnings and countless towns were flooded. You could barely turn on the TV without seeing images of streets transformed into cheap Venetian canals, half-submerged cars and traffic lights rising from murky waters. Root crops rotted in the fields, train services were canceled, landslips closed roads and hailstones the size of golf balls were said to have fallen in the Midlands. Everyone was blathering about that book, *Fifty Shades*, and the media made jokes about how wet the summer was, how gray. The sky was never blue; it was black and blue, storm clouds amassing in the distance whenever the sun tried to shine.

On days when the rain stopped, people glanced skyward with hopeful hearts, picturing barbecues at the weekend, a spot of gardening, maybe a walk across the Downs or a bike ride. But invariably, the world would darken and another deluge would descend.

Experts blamed the jet stream, but I could see it was actually my fault. I was creating chaos with my climaxes.

I'd started to suspect a connection, however, the notion seemed too crazy to divulge. But when my orgasm prompted a downpour fierce enough to activate a car alarm, Ray gave me a look suggesting he shared my concerns. "Okay, that's enough," he said. "We need to hold it right there."

For an awful moment, I thought he was dumping me. Then he explained what he meant, and I wondered if *I* should dump *him*.

"No orgasms?" I said. "None at all?"

"None."

"Not even a small one when no one's watching?"

"God's watching," said Ray.

"God's got better things to do than that," I replied.

Ray grinned and sat astride me, his cock angling up from his patch of straw-gold hair even though he'd only recently shot his load. I have to say, he wasn't my usual type. Tall and slender, he resembled Jesus, probably more so than Jesus did, although he had a neater beard and shorter hair. His eyes were deep brown, kind and dopey like a spaniel's, but he wasn't kind or dopey in bed. He liked to top, but his was a very geeky style of topping involving ropes, cuffs, vibes, new toys and tricks. He enjoyed the rigmarole, the complexities, and he liked to plot, making me feel I was a subject in a series of deeply unethical, scientific experiments. In his day-to-day life, he was a PhD student researching estuarine sedimentation and sea-level trends. Sometimes, I liked to pretend he was doing a PhD on me.

"Then quit for your country," he said. He took my wrists and lightly pinned my arms to the pillows above my head.

I laughed. "I'm not that patriotic, Ray."

"Okay then," he said. "Do it for me. Give me that amazing, precious part of you. Give me...give me the power of your orgasms. Let me be the one who tells you when you can and can't come."

"Hmm. It's a big ask."

Ray shrugged. "Wouldn't be worth doing otherwise."

I mulled it over. "Supposing I come accidentally? Say, when we're having sex and you're not concentrating and whoops, there I go."

"I won't let that happen."

"Well, supposing I come accidentally when you're not there? You know, say, I fall on my vibrator or something?"

"You won't let that happen." Ray's puppy-dog eyes were twinkling with excitement. I could practically hear the cogs of his brain whirring as he began contemplating the implications of his suggestion.

"I could lie to you," I said. "I could pretend I was obeying but in reality—"

"But I'd know," said Ray. "It would start raining."

"Gah!" I said. "There's no escape for me, is there?"

"Not much."

I sighed, defeated. "Still not convinced. Anyway, supposing it doesn't work and it keeps raining?"

Ray shrugged. "Nothing ventured, nothing gained."

We fell silent for a while. Outside the torrential downpour continued although the car alarm had stopped. That I had the power to improve the nation's weather was both a wonderful gift and an unwelcome responsibility. If only the gift were slightly different and involved, for example, not quitting orgasms but eating huge amounts of ice cream.

"Let's give it a whirl," said Ray. "Think how sexy it is. It's not just about the weather. It's about you making a sacrifice for me. And me having control over you and you wanting me to have control. Like this." He gave an emphatic shove, pressing my arms hard into the pillows. "And this." He placed one hand on top of the other, pinning my wrists with one grip, then reached behind himself to feel me between my thighs. He skimmed my clit. I was still sensitive from coming and I squealed, wriggling my hips beneath his weight. A burst of squally rain hurled itself at the window, as noisy as a handful of gravel being flung.

"I can make you do things any day of the week," Ray continued. He took both my hands, rested the left under his balls at an awkward angle, the right around his shaft. I did what was expected of me. His length twitched and flexed in my fist. "I can cuff you and torment you," Ray went on. "Force you because you like it. But just think. I'm not forcing you here. I'm *asking* you. No orgasms. And you agree and you stick with it."

He gave me a sly smile. "Because promises are stronger than leather."

I didn't reply. His cock was fully hard now. I kept working him with my hand, gazing down my torso at his flushed tip. Ray closed his eyes and groaned heavily. I wondered how he'd feel if I stopped. I didn't of course. I speeded up. He came on my stomach and tits, striping my skin with jizz. I was happy for him, as one is at the sight and sound of a lover's climax. I also felt a fleeting tug of jealousy. When would it be my turn again?

Horny doesn't even begin to cover it. Within a week I was practically clawing the walls, except the walls were the inside of my body. I ached to get outside of myself, to fly away via a dizzying, transcendent, cunt-clenching crisis.

It might have been bearable if Ray hadn't been such a goddamn tease. A change to our regular dates to accommodate my abstinence would have been fine; say, a few quiet nights in front of the telly, maybe meeting up with friends, going bowling or whatever. But oh, no. This was a man who got off on making me suffer. I should have seen it coming. Or rather, not.

The worst of it was, the weather held. Day after day, the sun beat down, ostensible proof that our experiment was working. In parks and gardens, flowers lifted their rain-battered heads. In town, people sat outside bars and cafes, gazing at the light, as stunned as newly emerged moles. The habit of glancing nervously at the sky was hard to break but gradually people started to seem happier and more relaxed, less sallow and hunched. *Summer's here!* proclaimed the headlines.

By week two, I was praying for rain so we could call the whole thing off. The heat caressed my skin. The sight of people in skimpy clothes was torture. The country stayed dry while my cunt was as wet as a rain cloud. Please tip it down, I thought.

But the sky remained flawlessly blue. As an additional cruelty, Ray started to tan. He'd been handsome enough when I'd met him, but the heat baked him golden, turning him into a bronzed, lanky, bewhiskered Adonis. I wanted him so badly. All of him.

He wasn't withholding himself from me; that was the killer. He would even fuck me and take me to the verge of climax, but he'd never allow me to get off. My feverish lust was never calmed. I became an unadulterated horndog, sexually obsessed and full of pent-up energy.

One evening in week three, we were seated on Ray's stone balcony, drinking ice-cold bottled beer and looking out over treetops, rooftops and tiny trains moving in and out of the distant station. The early evening sky was sliced with vapor trails, the horizon turning pink in the west. I was gripped with the need to climax. I wanted to jump Ray, strip him naked, ride his cock and come in a lunatic mess of slipperiness and screaming. At the very least, I wanted to maul and kiss him but I knew I had to resist. Molesting him would only culminate in exquisite agony with Ray once again taking me to the edge of orgasm then denying me my release. The obsession was addictive but it was a curious kind of addiction, one in which rather than give in to the thing I craved, I had to fight the longing for gratification, knowing my desire wouldn't be gratified and the urge would be worsened.

"People are saying the gardens need watering," I ventured.

"People are never satisfied," replied Ray. "Too much rain, they moan. Too much sun, they moan."

Jeez, even his voice made me horny. Well, everything made me horny. I'd listened to my neighbors fucking two nights previously and it had taken an enormous amount of willpower not to go and knock on their door and ask if I could have a ride. But sex-noises would have turned me on regardless. What was new was the hypersensitivity of my cunt. Showering and sitting in certain chairs became an erotic experience. New too was the way my body charged up at a whiff of aftershave in the street; at the sight of a woman uncrossing her legs or two sparrows splashing in a water bath; at the squelchy noise from a bottle of fabric conditioner being emptied by a man in the launderette; at the terrible painting of a conch shell in the dentist's waiting room resembling the pink frills of labia unfurling.

I was permanently aroused. I was a bitch in heat. I was desperately, tear-prickingly randy.

One muggy afternoon, I'd begged, "Please! Please let me!" as Ray had taken me to the brink with his fingers and some clit gel he'd bought. The gel warmed and tenderized me, its soft, tingling heat radiating into my groin, drawing sensation deeper. Ray held me there. The room darkened as the sun disappeared behind a cloud. My thighs were starting to quiver. I was moments away. I thought he was finally going to let me go, and the heavens would open. I was on the edge of relief, about to bring an end to the oppressive humidity. But Ray pulled back. I could feel his breath still warm on my folds. He pushed a finger inside me, gave me a hard, fast stroke then withdrew. He flicked my clit. Beneath his finger, I was a fat, slippery bead. I bucked, searching for him.

"Please," I wailed.

"Don't let me down," he said. He kissed my swollen clit.

Oh, dear god. Every nerve trembled beneath the touch of his lips. "Please."

"You know you don't mean that." He licked me once, twice, teasing me with his careful tongue. I swear I could feel the bumps of his taste buds on my taut, raw clit.

"Ray, I can't stand it. Please let me come."

He laughed softly. For a few moments, he said nothing. He

blew a stream of cool air on my flesh. "How's the gel?" he asked.
"It's made my mouth go a bit weird."

"Yeah," I said. "Good. Fading a bit now."

Soft light filled the room as the clouds dissipated.

"Well, then," said Ray. "I'd better apply some more, hadn't
I?"

And so it went on with Ray taking me to the threshold of
ecstasy before pulling back only to take me there again. I imagined the rain clouds high in the sky, weighted with wetness
and not knowing if they were coming or going. I felt sorry for
them because, unlike me, they presumably weren't getting much
enjoyment from this.

Because yes, even though our experiment was an ordeal of
fleshly frugality, the days of uncertainty and submission to Ray's
control were also infuriatingly wonderful. I was coasting on a
sexual high, permeated by a dizzying euphoria and as horny as
a teenager.

I hadn't realized what a sadist my new boyfriend was until
I'd granted him control of my orgasms. I hadn't realized, either,
what a thrill I'd get from doing as I was told, from obeying
Ray's orders even when he wasn't there. Alone at night, I didn't
once touch myself, my hands as good as tied by the promise
that I'd made. I felt as if he were always with me, close by my
side, guarding and protecting. I was captivated by the game and
charmed by Ray's bossiness. He'd wrapped me in magic, and I'd
fallen under his spell.

The Met Office was baffled. An "unprecedented heat wave" it
said, as experts admitted long-range forecasts had been wrong.
Despite the rainfall earlier in the year, a drought was rumored
to be imminent. Ray was totally unfazed by this, so excited
by his orgasm-control experiments he seemed prepared to let

reservoir levels fall. I was torn between wanting to come, wanting to please and wanting the lunacy of unslaked lust to continue.

We came to our senses one dazzling afternoon when we walked past a construction worker hosing down the hoardings edging a building site. Hosepipe in hand, the guy blasted water at the dusty plastic wall, the jet fierce enough to bounce back a cloud of spray onto the other side of the road where we walked. Ahead of us the air shimmered, a veiled rainbow trapped in its diaphanous haze. As we walked on, the mist draped itself on our skin, so cool and light. We laughed. I tasted the spray. Its sudden chill refreshed my mouth. I felt as if I'd swallowed the rainbow, its myriad of colors dissolving on my tongue like sorbet stripes of raspberry, peach, lemon, lime, blueberry, blackberry and plum.

"Damn, that felt good," said Ray.

I shivered with pleasure, my skin coated in moisture.

That evening, Ray was as cruel as ever in denying me my release but when he left me in the morning he said, "Tonight's the night. Tonight you get to come."

The sky must have heard him because later, I opened my curtains to see blue-gray clouds in the distance. I was in a tizz of anticipation all day. The clouds swelled, increasingly menacing, and the air was swampy with humidity. Was it really going to rain? Was I really going to remember what it felt like to climax?

When I walked to Ray's that evening, the light held a dark glint of pewter. My skin was clammy. Sweat slid on the back of my neck. I was bloated between my thighs, my cunt a burden of tissue rubbing and slipping with every stride I took. My juices spilled from me. The birds were noisy and gulls circled, unsettled as if they sensed imminent danger. Sounds were muffled, my sandals thudding dully on the ground. I thought I heard a distant rumble of thunder.

"Let's get you out of these wet things," said Ray when I arrived. I was damp with perspiration, but I knew he was referring specifically to my underwear. As if to back up his comment, he reached under my skirt and stroked the sodden pouch of my gusset. His touch sparked a bolt of need fierce enough to make me weak at the knees.

"Don't make me wait too long," I breathed, lifting my arms so he could remove my top.

He tugged off his own tee, baring his honey-bronze torso. I stroked his sweat-moist skin as he unclasped my bra and scattered kisses over my breasts. I felt woozy. When we were naked, I was instructed to sit in the armchair, legs wide apart.

Ray looked down at me, big, brown eyes roaming over my body before focusing on the glossy slit at the juncture of my thighs. His gaze was like a touch, inciting my flesh to arousal. He dropped to his knees and printed kisses along my legs, moving higher toward my inner thighs.

"How long has it been?" Gently, he toyed with my flushed, tender lips, watching my expression as he opened me with a single finger. He slid along my wet seam, nudging at my entrance then edging toward my clit.

I groaned and wriggled. "Too fucking long."

He kept stroking me. "Four weeks and two days," he said, full of pride. "Well done."

I groaned again, pained to hear how long I'd gone without.

For several more minutes, Ray teased me while I writhed and whimpered. Finally, he slid two fingers into my wetness. The room grew suddenly darker, shadows cast by cloud not dusk. Ray rubbed me inside, leaning over me to smear kisses against my lips, his buried fingers picking up speed, his erection nudging at my body. Before long, he was giving me a curled-finger fuck, half-thrusting, half-tugging while his thumb bumped my clit.

"Yes, there, there. I'm going to—"

Instantly, he eased off. "No, you don't. Not yet."

"No!" I protested. "You said I could. You said tonight—"

"Shhh!" He dropped back to kneel between my spread legs again. Looking up at my face, he rolled my clit with excruciating slowness. "When I'm ready," he said.

I should have known he would spin out my torment, building me up again to that mad pitch where I imagined I could do serious criminal damage if only it meant I got to come. Strung out on the crazy back and forth of being indulged and denied, I never knew if this time, if this moment when the delicate tremors tightened in my thighs, would be the one when I'd be allowed to let go and ride the orgasmic wave.

In the end, Ray told me. His fingers were inside me and he raised his head, lips glistening with my fluids, to say, "Any time. Any time you want to come." He lowered his mouth to my clit again. The touch of his tongue felt like something I could finally trust. No more games. A huge pressure was lifted from me, that psychological release urging on my fast-approaching sexual release.

I gasped as Ray's tongue danced, my pleasure rising steeply until I was there, poised on the brink of no return. For a moment, the world stopped spinning, the universe held its breath and then I was crying out as my orgasm poured through me, gripping and tumbling, over and over. My body jerked and quivered, racked by an intensity I'd never known before. I floated outside myself, became formless and vast, as big as the sky. Lost to ecstasy, my senses scattered and I melted into Ray's mouth, clutching his hair, my back arching as my cunt liquefied.

Right on cue, rain crackled beyond the window. Lightning

lashed the gloomy room. The sky gave a low, rolling groan as if returning a distorted echo of my bliss. I bumped gently back to earth and sank into floppiness. Ray sat back on his heels, his cock angled high. Outside, the rain kept on clattering and roaring, flashes of lightning chased by booming thunder as a storm of biblical proportions moved closer.

"Wow," murmured Ray, gazing at the half-raised window.

I said nothing. I barely had strength to breathe. The noise of the downpour was immense, the rain bringing a welcome, earth-scented freshness into the room.

After a while, Ray said, "If I'd known you wanted to come this badly, I'd have built an ark."

I laughed softly. "Good for the gardens."

The room exploded with a nanosecond of light.

"And the reservoirs," said Ray.

"And umbrella sales."

Thunder ripped the sky apart. The building trembled.

Ray kissed me between my thighs. "Looks like we're in for a wet spell."

THE CUSTOMER'S WAITING

Giselle Renarde

My butch-crush Levy worked in a cage downstairs—down in the deep, dark, scary basement underneath the big, bright, shiny department store. She had the kind of job most people have never heard of: she fixed merchandise customers broke or returned, and she shipped manufacturers products that were still under warrantee. Anything she couldn't fix or get repaired, she wrote off.

Levy was supposed to ditch the busted goods, but she went against corporate regulations and kept them for parts. Management probably knew, but they were too scared to scold her. Levy always said that's why they had her working in a cage—they could lock her in there like a rabid dog if she ever got out of control. You wouldn't know it to look at her, but Levy had a great sense of humour. Nobody knew the real her. That's because she scared everyone shitless.

But not me. I wasn't afraid. Or, if I was, the fear was tempered so much by attraction that it only pumped up my desire to seek out the dyke downstairs and rattle her cage. I daydreamed about Levy constantly. I looked for any excuse to go down there.

Me? I worked the sales floor, part-time because management claimed nothing else was available. Not that I believed a word they said. I knew better than to trust "the man," even when the man was a group of nattering women, and even if that group brought in less than thirty thousand each for managing the hell-hole they called a department store.

Management assigned me to the sports department even though I knew less than nothing about hockey sticks and tennis rackets. Evening shifts were the worst. I had to work them alone, which was daunting until I realized "alone" didn't just mean without other staff members, it meant without any customers either. People had better things to do at nine thirty on a Wednesday night than buy badminton birdies. *Shuttlecocks.* Levy taught me that word last week. I'd covered my lips and let them have their naughty smile.

I was daydreaming about Levy stripping me bare and testing out one of the "neck massagers" from health and beauty on my naked body when a customer with a big bouffant hairdo approached me. She was way too well dressed to be shopping in a dump like this but, hey, it took all kinds.

The woman glanced down at my name tag and said, "Excuse me...Asian?"

"Ashlin," I corrected her.

The woman gave me a confused sort of smile and pointed to a fishing rod inside the Plexiglas case. She started asking questions, but it was all Greek to me. I didn't know anything about fishing.

So, I figured this was as good a time as any to hit up Levy for sports information. I told the woman with the big hairdo that I'd have to check with an associate. She didn't seem too pleased about that, but I was pleased—pleased I'd be seeing my crush in thirty seconds flat.

Tearing my uniform smock over my head, I ran through the store and swung open the staff-only door. One of the forklift guys in delivery made some comment about my skirt, which was rule-defiantly short. Any other day I might have cared, but I was about to see Levy. Stupid guys could say whatever they damn well pleased.

I rushed into the back staircase and popped two buttons on my blouse. Nobody else worked in the basement. Just Levy. No one else would see.

In my wedge heels, I had to be careful walking down those slatted metal stairs. It really was scary in the basement. Everything was either concrete or metal, and the only sign of life came from Levy's blaring headphones. She obviously hadn't noticed me yet, and I gripped the metal railing, just watching her work.

There was something about dykes who looked like truck drivers that really turned me on. That was Levy's style—dark blue pants like mechanics wore, and an unbuttoned short-sleeve shirt over a tank top. Her sandy hair was about shoulder length, but she always wore it back in a ponytail, with a baseball cap that said MACK and had a bulldog on it.

Just the sight of her made my pussy pulse. I was so wet she could probably fist me in one go, if she wanted to.

And that was the kicker: so far, she hadn't expressed any interest in me. None. At all. Every shift, I dressed a little more femme—brighter lipstick, shorter skirt, higher heels. Anything to grab her attention.

It took about a minute and a half to work up the courage to call her from the bottom of the stairs, but she didn't hear me. I crept toward her cage until I was close enough to weave my fingers through and shake it. Levy jumped almost a foot off the ground, turning simultaneously and tearing off her head-phones.

She was obviously scared, but she covered it up, yelling, "What are you trying to do, give me a heart attack?"

I apologized coyly while she turned off her music, then posed the big-haired customer's question. Levy came up with an answer, easy as pie. When I didn't leave, just peered through the cage like a lost puppy, she stared at me, hard, unyielding, and finally said, "The customer's waiting."

What did I care? I just shrugged and kept staring, smiling like an idiot. I was really good at saying stupid things to girls I liked. With Levy, I usually complimented her hat or her top or her rainbow bootlaces, but none of that had worked so far. When I asked if I could come into her cage, I didn't expect her to say yes. In fact, when she did, I thought I'd heard her wrong.

The door had a latch on it like the one on the gate to my parents' backyard. She flipped it, opened the cage and yanked me in. Her eyes kept asking me what I wanted, but she didn't say a word. That's when I saw them: two different models of "neck massagers" from the sales floor. They were right on top of Levy's big shop-teacher desk, just waiting to be played with.

I picked one up, and Levy shot me a look like she didn't want me touching her stuff. I didn't mind those looks. She gave them to me all the time. I didn't even care if she didn't like me yet, because I knew she would, in time. Most people didn't like me at first. It took a little while, but I won them over with subtle charm.

Waving the smaller massager at Levy, I asked, "What's the deal with this thing? Did a customer return it?"

"No," Levy scoffed. "We don't accept returns on stuff like that. Didn't you read the employee manual?"

I shrugged again, hiding my smile. She was so mean to me and I loved it, because it was the meanness of an eight-year-old pulling a little girl's pigtails. Levy liked me and didn't want to admit it, not even to herself. When I put the massager back on her desk, she told me the products were for her own "personal interest."

I couldn't have asked for better fodder for teasing. "Oh, so that's why you work such long hours, huh? Management thinks you're so industrious, but really you're just sitting down here with your pants around your ankles."

"Shut up," she said, turning her back on me. She fished through her cubbyholes full of screws and packing materials until she found what she was looking for. When she turned to face me, Levy had a packet of cable ties in hand.

I'd broken her. She would top me. I'd finally won.

"Stand against the cage if you're so clever," Levy said. "Feet apart, arms in the air. Like a snow angel."

I felt giddy as I got into position, spreading my legs for her. When she came close to me, I could smell the basement on her clothing. Damp and concrete dust. It made me want to sneeze, but I held it in. Levy probably didn't want my spit and snot all over her.

She bound me to the cage with a series of cable ties—down one arm, down the other. She put them on over my silky blouse so I could feel the pressure of them against my wrist, my forearm, my elbow, but the plastic wasn't biting into my skin. That was a nice touch. She bound my ankles to the cage as well, and when it occurred to me that I was trapped, my heart began to race.

"Thank you," I said.

"I haven't done anything yet."

"You have no idea..."

Levy went to her desk and picked up the wand. It was one of

those Hitachi doodads. I'd never actually used one. She plugged it into an extension cord and thumped toward me. Her cage was built on a raised wooden platform, and every step boomed through the basement.

"So this is what you want, eh?" Levy tapped the massager against her palm like a baseball bat. The end was bulbous and rounded; no way could it fit in my pussy. Way too big. I tried to close my legs, but of course they were secured with cable ties.

When I didn't answer, Levy asked, "If I do this, will you finally stop coming down here and making googly eyes at me?"

I smiled and bit my bottom lip.

"Well?"

"No," I said. "I'll keep coming back. I like you too much."

She rolled her eyes and sort of said, "Pfft," but I saw a grin on her lips. She wanted me. She loved the sight of me strung up against her cage, helpless, just waiting for her to do whatever she wanted.

That big toy in her hand buzzed to life, emitting a low hum. I felt all squirmy inside, but I couldn't squirm. I was stuck to the cage. My knees felt weak, but I bolstered my legs, planting my heels hard into the ground. If I let them go, I'd be strung up by my arms and the cable ties would cut my skin right through my shirt.

"You don't know me," Levy said. Her steel-toed boots touched the tips of my wedge heels. "How can you trust me?"

"I just do," I told her. There was no reason behind it.

"Enough to let me tie you up at work where anybody could walk down those stairs and find us?"

I would have shrugged, but I couldn't move my shoulders. "Nobody ever comes down here but me. And you."

Levy leaned in, right close to my ear, and said, "They will when they hear your little-girl screams." Her breath was so hot it made me sweat. I could feel little beads building under my breasts, soaking into my bra.

"Did you think I would touch you?" Levy asked over the vibrator's buzz. It was touching my skirt, making the fabric ripple. "Did you come down here thinking I'd eat your tight little pussy?"

When I didn't reply, Levy lifted my skirt with the buzzing head of the massager. She traced it up and down my inner thighs, but I could already feel the low vibrations in my cunt. I kind of wished she would touch me, just so she'd see how wet I'd become. It never took long. I could slick my panties on the bus just thinking about Levy.

And they were super-slick now. I felt my juice mashing against my pulpy pussy when Levy pushed the vibe against my panties. I felt that first, the vibrations second. Once they hit, my knees buckled and I hung from the cable ties.

Too many sensations all at once. Intense buzzing against my clit. It travelled down my legs like the blood in my veins. The pain of those cable ties sliced through my arms. I arched forward, but that put too much pressure on my wrists. My hands started feeling numb, so I forced myself to stand properly. There was no other option.

"How's that?" Levy asked as she stroked my pussy with the massager's giant head. "Feel good? Feel nice?"

"Yeah," I panted. "Very good. Very nice."

I could hardly handle the vibrations through my underwear, but I still wanted to feel that buzzing thing right against my flesh. I wanted her to open me up like a gift and set that vibe flush to my clit. It throbbed in there, all hidden beneath folds of flesh and fabric. Even tucked away like that, it felt huge and ripe as a cherry hot off the tree. I imagined Levy taking it in her mouth and sucking, juice running down her chin and dripping onto the floorboards. Just the thought made me arch and whine. Sometimes my mind was more powerful than any sex toy.

And other times sex toys won the day.

Levy stuck the vibe between her own thighs and held it there tight. I could see by the look of ecstasy in her eyes that the vibrations were riding through the seam of her pants, finding her clit just like they'd found mine. Pulling my skirt up over my hips, she pushed forward, driving the head against my pussy. She unbuttoned my blouse, clumsily, like an animal. Tearing my breasts from the cups of my bra, she bent down and sucked my tits so zealously I shrieked. "Christ, that hurts!"

She didn't stop. She went at my tits like the thing between her legs drove her impulses. Levy had been so focused on sucking and thumbing and slapping my tits that I thought maybe she'd forgotten about my pussy. But no. She shoved my panties down and they locked in place against my spread thighs. She pushed them again, but they rolled in on themselves, except for the gusset, which was spread wide and slick with pussy juice.

Levy growled, and I could feel that low rumble in my belly alongside the deep vibrations of the massager. She pushed my lips aside with the vibe, like opening the curtains to a sunny day. Pressing her cock-vibe against my clit, she fucked it, and the sensation was so brutal and so wonderful it booted me right out of my body.

I watched from above as she kissed me, kissed me as hard as she'd sucked my nipples. My breasts were now slammed against her chest, her hat sliding to the side, my back pushed into the wire cage. The cable ties made my arms scream, but I couldn't speak. Her tongue pushed past my teeth and rooted around my mouth like it was searching for something. I couldn't think, couldn't move, couldn't do anything but let her pound that vibe against my swollen clit and kiss me crazy.

"You like that, eh?" She grabbed the vibe and mashed it in tight circles around my clit. "Yeah, you like it."

Levy grabbed my tit with the other hand, pinching my nipple and tugging it. God, it hurt so much. She'd made me sensitive by sucking my breasts. Now my nipples were red and raw and every time she yanked one a big sound built inside of me. It was trapped in my throat just now, but it was coming. *Coming.*

"The customer's waiting," she said. "She's gonna be so fucking mad she'll find a manager and tell 'em what a bad girl you are."

Stealing the vibe away from my cunt, Levy turned up the power and whacked me with it, square in the clit. I winced, but I wanted more.

She held the vibe against my clit, and I struggled to get away from it. I couldn't of course, but the pulse was too strong to bear. I tried folding in on myself, but that didn't work. I was bound open. I couldn't close.

"Customer's gonna tell the boss you should be fired." Levy whacked me in the cunt again, and followed that with a slap— her hand on my tits. The sting of it coursed through me and I gritted my teeth to keep from screaming. "Boss'll come looking, find you strung up in the basement with a massager hanging out of your cunt. You'll be speaking in tongues, me long gone, you strung up and desperate."

My mind was melting, and still I said, "That thing would never fit inside my pussy."

A challenge.

Levy didn't play any more word games with me. She just slid the vibe down and pressed it up against my slit. My pussy was too tight for that thing, and still I wanted it to fill me. I wanted the vibrations inside of me.

"Ain't gonna work, little girl." Levy pushed regardless, and my pussy lips spread wide. The vibrations were everywhere. I could feel them in my asshole, even though nothing was touching it. I could feel them in my toes.

I looped my fingers back around the cage, clinging to the wire. "Fuck me. Put it in. Do it."

Levy eased the massager up into my slit, but she was daintier about this than she'd been with anything else. Constant pressure. My cunt was so slick, the vibrations so severe, that I thought we just might get there.

She twisted it this way and that, and my pussy hugged that thing, sucking it in. I wanted it. I wanted it. My legs were spread. Little resistance. I told my pussy to be good, be nice, let the big bad toy inside, and by some miracle it worked. The bulbous head entered my cunt and my pussy lips closed around it.

Levy turned the vibrations up to maximum, and I lost it. My whole body was a vibrator, running from within. I rattled the cage, screaming as I bucked back and shook. Fuck, I couldn't move. So much blood had drained from my hands I could hardly feel them, but I could sure as hell feel the cable ties biting into my flesh. I felt like I was being electrocuted. I could hardly open my eyes, but when I did I saw Levy smiling like the cat that got the canary. She could resist all she liked, but she wanted this just as much as I did.

"You've had enough," she said, when my knees buckled and I couldn't recover.

"No, no, no!" I tried to right myself, but it was just impossible. I looked down at my skirt pulled up, my panties pulled down. The white massager hung like a cock between my legs, trailing a white cord attached to an orange extension. I could hardly believe this was happening. "No, I want more. I can take more."

Levy worked the bulb head slowly from my cunt, blowing cool breath against my clit all the while. When it was out of me, the relief was as tangible as anything I could hold in my hand. Levy stared at the gloss of my cunt coating the vibe. She turned it off and then set it to my lips, pressing until I opened them and licked my own pussy juice from the toy.

"That's good," Levy said in a lullaby voice. "Good girl."

When she cut me down, I fell against her and she struggled to grab something soft to kneel on—a plush, toy department hippopotamus with one eye missing.

Levy stayed there on the floor with me and let me lean my weight against hers. My hands got pins and needles, and I shook them out but they hurt like hell.

"You think your customer's still waiting?" she asked.

"What customer?"

"You came down to ask about a fishing rod, said you had a customer. Unless you were making that up."

I laughed. "No, that was true. But I'm sure she's left by now. Hey, maybe I *will* get fired!" The thought enlivened me somewhat.

Levy pulled a box of mini–chocolate bars off her shelves and tore one open for me. I tried to grab it, but my fingers hadn't come back to life yet, so she fed it to me bite by bite. I'd never felt so cared for in all my life.

"I'd miss you if you were gone," Levy said. She ate some chocolate, too, and my belly warmed with sugar and compliments. "It's my favorite part of the day, you know, when you slide down those stairs in your pretty little outfits and your big-ass shoes."

I bit my lip but couldn't keep the laughter inside. She pulled me close on the plush hippo and we ate chocolate together.

"You're my favorite part of the day, too," I said, though I was pretty sure she knew it already. "You're my favorite part of life."

The customer might have been waiting until the store closed for the night, but I would never know. I spent all that time gorging on chocolate and flirting with Levy, locked away in the cage of her subterranean lair.

BOUND
BY SIGHT

J. Sinclaire

I bring men home. Not daily. But often enough for my crotchety landlady to give me the stink eye. She's in the apartment below mine, an unfortunate circumstance that means she is privy to all sorts of muffled sounds coming from my bedroom at all hours of the day. My needs have no set timetable, and his gaze is upon me no matter the time.

I know he's there. Comfortably stationed in the building across the way. Watching me. He is the reason I leave the curtains open. It's an understatement to say it gives me a thrill to know he sees me in these sticky, damp happenstances with whoever has piqued my interest recently.

Today it was the grocer's assistant. The strapping lad who's still saving up for higher education, despite having finished high school more than three years ago. His blowhard manager regularly reminds him of this. Perhaps a decade my junior but still fair game. Normally too shy to even make eye contact, I managed to draw his attention with well-timed dips and bends for my purchases in flattering outfits. The first few times I let him steal his glances but the last, I met his gaze once he'd raised it past my chest. His blush was immediate and encompassed his entire torso not covered by his uniform. I decided that was the opportune time to make my move.

As the store is only a block from my home, I coerced his assistance in carrying home a last-minute purchase I did not need in the slightest: a case of bottled water. He was hesitant at first, unsure of whether it was allowed, but when he questioned the aforementioned manager, I could tell by his smirk and nod that he realized it would be greatly beneficial for the lad to help a weak little lady like myself with her chores.

My arms full of groceries I did require, I walked beside him at a slow pace, enjoying the tension in the air. My red curls draped over my bare shoulders to touch the hem of my aquamarine strapless dress that seemed to defy gravity as it clung to my breasts. Though petite, I had ample curves and a trim waist, a miracle of genetics that I did nothing to nurture. My pale skin had not yet had a chance to burn this spring and it was a stark contrast to the vivid color of my dress and hair. I caught him watching my body undulate with each step and smiled a bit more.

"What's your name?" I asked, my voice already breathier than normal from the possibilities running through my brain.

He glanced at my face and then at the ground again, his brown mop of hair covering his eyes. "David."

I let my eyes wander over him: tall and lanky but with more strength than you'd think by the way he easily propped the case of water on his shoulder. His drab green uniform shirt had lifted a bit to expose part of his stomach, well defined but with a nice layer of bitable chub. His black pants were held up with a well-worn belt, the last notch made by hand yet not quite tight enough as his pants still hung onto his hips loosely. His hip bones jutted out just enough to make me visualize using them as handles while I serviced his cock on my knees.

"Nice to meet you, David." I responded, exhaling as I said his name. "I'm Audrey. I appreciate you taking the time to help me carry that home. I know you're not supposed to."

He cleared his throat before replying. "No problem." He was looking at me but having difficulty meeting my eyes. His tall stature made it even easier for him to stare down my dress, and I smirked again at my obvious influence on him.

We walked the rest of the way in silence, which wasn't very long at all. As I reached in my purse for my keys, he started to lower the case onto the front step and make his exit. I caught his wrist before he raised it in good-bye and we met eyes.

"Come in. Please. At least for a glass of water."

He paused for a moment, licking his lower lip nervously before nodding. I smiled and went back to the task of opening the door. He picked up the water again as I let us into the front foyer and then led him toward the stairs up to my apartment. Switching the bags over to one hand, I used the other to grasp the edge of my skirt up to my thigh as we climbed. While helpful in ensuring I didn't trip over my dress it also showed my shapely legs to David, whose eyes were locked on them with every step. I lifted the hem higher as I reached the landing, turning the corner and pirouetting to face him with one leg up on a step.

"Are you okay? It's not too heavy?" I queried, certain that in this pose he could easily see my bare lips peeking out beneath my skirt. Maybe even the small tuft of ginger hair at the top of my mound.

He'd frozen on the stairs and was staring at my thighs. Even though he was slightly bent over, I could see the bulge beginning to rise in his pants.

"David?" I prodded when he didn't respond. He looked up at

my face finally, his expression dreamy and bewildered. "Are you okay carrying that up the stairs?" I repeated, and he snapped back to reality, his face immediately flushing red.

"Oh. Uh. Yes, I'm fine." He didn't sound fine. He sounded confused but swayed by his erection to ignore the oddness of my behavior.

I smiled at him and continued the climb, reaching the top of the stairs and opening my door quickly lest he try to run again. Glancing over my shoulder at his still bewildered but hungry eyes, I realized that would not be a problem. He followed me into the kitchen, a large space that shared with the living room. As the structure was not originally built for residences, there were large, boxy windows all along one side of the apartment, including the bedroom. Great for natural light and voyeurs. My watcher's apartment was the only one with a full view of mine though, so at least that possibility was limited.

Dropping the bags of groceries on the counter, I pointed toward an empty spot on the ground near the windows for him to put the case of water before grabbing a glass and opening up the fridge. Pouring him a glass of ice-cold water, I swung the door shut with a quick bump of my hip and walked over to him. Standing close enough to make him back up against the counter, I coyly looked up at his lips as I handed him the glass. His hand was a bit shaky as he took it from me and for a second, I wondered if I was being cruel to someone so seemingly innocent.

The moment passed.

He took a drink and I moved closer to him, my hands on his belt as I started to undo his pants. My touch surprised him and he choked on some of the water he'd barely managed to swallow. Making reassuring sounds, I put one hand on his chest until he calmed again while the other relieved him of his pants. Any doubts regarding his level of interest were assuaged by his erection and the look in his eyes. He stared down at me; pleading, longing, mixed with a bit of bewilderment under a strong foundation of desire. Biting my lip, I ran my palm over him through his underwear from the tip of his head down to cup his balls, watching his reaction as I did so. He did not disappoint. Leaning against the counter, his head tipped back and he arched his body toward me.

This boy just kept making me smile. Releasing his balls, I hooked my fingers into his underpants and pulled them off slowly, lowering myself to pepper his stomach with light kisses on the way down. I took a moment to settle onto my knees and admire his cock. Large, as I'd suspected, though it was truly impressive in girth. Thick and solid, it was an intimidating sight for my jaw. Luckily, my recent succession of gentlemen callers had ensured it was not an impossible task.

Glancing over my shoulder quickly to confirm our positions relative to the windows beside us, I looked up at him and locked eyes before touching his shaft with my tongue. His body shuddered and his grip on the counter behind him tightened. I licked a line from his base to his head, my tongue swirling about the tip before pulling away.

"David, I'd like to suck your cock for a long while but I want you to fuck me after. Will that be a problem?" I was subtly questioning his stamina, not his intentions. He understood and quickly nodded his approval.

My lips enveloped him before he could finish nodding. Sliding just the tip of him inside me forced my mouth open almost completely but after a few strokes down to the hilt, I got used to it. Working him at a steady pace with my tongue, I imagined how he would feel thrusting into my cunt. My body's reaction was immediate, my pussy flushing hot with desire and with it, words in my mind.

You'd like that, wouldn't you? You dirty bitch. I could almost hear my watcher's voice as if he were beside me. His words were potent. I eagerly sucked on David's dick harder and faster. *Sucking dick and aching to be fucked like the slut you are.*

I moaned as much as the cock between my lips allowed and moved my hand beneath my dress to my already wet mound. Teasing my clit, I thought of the man that started this all.

He had dark hair and perpetual stubble that made him look rugged but not unkempt. His eyes were hazel and the first thing I noticed when he'd introduced himself. Connor. He'd chatted me up at the coffee shop down the street. Coy, easy flirting that quickly led to dinner plans for that evening. I was not afraid to pursue a man if I was interested in sex, but he was more persuasive and easy to say yes to than most. Dinner was electric, and his hand on my knee for the briefest moment caused such a reaction I was practically dragging him up the stairs to my apartment. By the time we burst through my front door, I did literally drag him toward the bedroom, but he stopped me in the living room.

He kissed me deeply, passionately and calmed my frenzied movements. He was intoxicating and it took me a moment to realize he'd pulled away to look at me. His arm around my waist, he walked us over to the window and pointed to the windows of the building across the way.

"That is where I live," he stated bluntly and watched my reaction. My confusion and then dawning realization cleared the lust from my mind. Moving out of his grip and with narrowed eyes I replied, "You live in that apartment across from mine?"

He nodded, his expression blank.

I considered the implications. He could obviously see into my home. I barely knew this man. But he intrigued me.

"Do you watch me?" I asked him bluntly and that elicited a smile.

"No. I have seen you in passing, with a man or making coffee, but I have not watched you."

He paused, not in hesitation but I think for more dramatic impact.

"But I would like to."

The lust returned full force. It was not a kink I was aware I had, and I was still not sure it would be something I'd enjoy. But based on how easily the idea had turned me on, I was willing to try. For whatever reason, I believed he was honest about not watching me previously. He'd not done anything to send up red flags, though this would obviously need to be handled carefully.

I closed the gap between us before responding.

"I think we should start with touch before we discuss sight."

His hands were on me immediately and he proved to be *very* good with the touching. Stumbling into the bedroom, he stripped me down quickly and pushed me onto the bed, going to work with his fingers and tongue. He built my pleasure slowly and methodically until I was begging him for release. I came so hard I nearly lost consciousness...and then I came some more. Before I could catch my breath, he flipped me onto my stomach and slid inside me from behind. He fucked me roughly, pinning me down in place, and started asking me questions. Simple ones at first, that became more aggressive the more I complied.

"Does my cock feel good? Do you like it? Are you a good slut who likes to be fucked hard?" I agreed to it all, my orgasms tearing through me, each accusation heightening the pleasure.

By the end of it, I was a wet, obedient mess. I'd had rough sex before but his demeanor, his control of the situation brought me to new heights. The idea of him watching me thrilled me now.

I was coyer when I presented it to him. I walked to my ward-
robe and donned my favorite red silk robe before returning to
where he was sprawled on the bed.

"You can watch me…but I have terms. I will close my curtains
if I need privacy. If I decide to end our arrangement, I'll hang
this robe on the window and you will respect my wishes. If I see
you glancing my way after that, I'll call the cops."

I was matter-of-fact, and he smiled at my blunt approach.

"Perfectly reasonable. I have a request, if you'd be so kind…"

I smirked at him then nodded, trying to ignore the throbbing
between my thighs triggered by the look in his eyes.

"I want to see you fuck. Whomever. Whenever. My business
keeps me at home and distraction is always appreciated. Your
body is enchanting and to watch it at lustful work…" He trailed
off as he eyed my body and then reached for me again.

Lying back on the bed, he lifted me onto his cock so I was
facing away from him in a riding position. Grasping my arms
behind me, he bound me easily with one hand as he gave me
instructions.

"Fuck yourself with my cock. Yes, that's it. Grind me, push
me inside as deep as you can. Faster. Show me how much you
want my dick." He growled the words in my ear. I brought
myself to orgasm as I rode him, collapsing against him as I came
down. He reached his other hand around me to grasp my neck
under my jaw, pulling my lips close against his.

"Did I say you could stop?" he asked bluntly. I shook my
head no as much as his grip allowed and started to move my
hips again. Being pressed against him made it nearly impossible
to maneuver and after a few moments of struggling, he stilled
my movement. Pulling me up slightly, he arched his hips away
before thrusting into me. Slowly. Maddeningly.

"If you can't fuck me properly, you'll need to learn." His

tone was impatient, bored even. I bit my lip to stifle a moan as he casually prodded my G-spot. "You'll learn to give as good as you take. Do you want more?"

His hips crashed against mine, filling me completely, and I choked out, "Yes!" I could feel his smile against my neck as he nibbled my skin. He sped up the pace, fucking me harder but keeping me bound against him. Whispering lusty commands and thoughts at me the entire time. We rushed to climax together and by the end of it, we settled on our terms.

He would watch me when I let him. I would let him more often than I'd planned to. I started to bring home more men. Sex was better with his voice in my head and his covert control over me.

Which is why I'm sucking David's cock in my kitchen. Well, it isn't the only reason, but it does make it more tantalizing. In my reminiscing, I missed the change in his moans from pleasant to urgent. He's close to coming but I'm not done with him yet.

Lifting my mouth from him, I pull my dripping fingers from my cunt and slide them over his cock. He looks down, watching as I tug my dress off my breasts, exposing them to the cool air. My nipples harden, light pink but still vivid against my pale skin. I shift so I can nestle his wet dick between my breasts, pumping him back and forth slowly for a few minutes.

He lowers one hand to cup my face and I relent, knowing I'm just making it more difficult for him to hold on. Standing up slowly, he drops his lips to mine and kisses me with a hunger that belies his shy attitude. In a whirl of movement, he lifts me in the air and onto the edge of the kitchen counter. Pushing my dress up to my waist, he takes his turn on his knees and laps at me greedily.

Oh the exuberance of youth. He's trying his best but is

obviously new to this act. I give him a few minutes, reaching into my nearby purse to grab a condom before pulling him back up against me. He seems a bit confused by my actions but catches on quickly as I unroll the condom down his cock in one smooth motion. My counter is the perfect height for him and he prods the entrance of my pussy excitedly before using his hand to guide.

He slams into me and I gasp, filled by him immediately. He cups my face again and worriedly asks if I'm okay. I nod, savoring the feel of him. The fullness. I slowly open my eyes though I don't recall having closed them. My nails dig into his shoulder and side as I respond.

"Harder."

He grins and the true, mischievous man hiding under the shy exterior shows himself. He thrusts again, wrapping his arms around my lower back and ass to stop me from sliding back on the counter from the force of it. I bite my lip. It's almost too much but as I'd suspected, he's much more talented with his cock than he is with his mouth.

His pace is slow but hard, every thrust making me cry out louder than before. Connor's voice returns, tormenting me.

What a good slut you are. Taking every inch of his cock. Over and over again. Isn't it time for you to come? Fucking come for me.

I'm sent over the edge in a matter of moments, clutching at his body as my muscles shudder their release. David looks surprised but content when I've come down enough to open my eyes again. He's slowed his pace and teases me with just the tip of his head drifting inside me.

I moan and shift toward him. He seems to decide he likes this turn of events, where he's able to make me squirm instead of vice versa, and he pushes me down onto the cool counter. He holds my hips in place and reaches over to grip my breasts occasionally as he builds up the pace slowly. He still teases me with shallow thrusts but after a few minutes of squirming, he's back to pounding me hard and deep.

The counter is not quite long enough for my entire body and my head hangs over the side. My breasts bounce with every thrust. I turn to look out the window and see Connor. Watching me. A thrill runs down my spine. He's sitting in a chair, in shadow but lit enough I can see him running his hand over the front of his pants. If you weren't looking for him though, he'd be hard to spot.

I watch him watch me and listen to David's grunts growing louder. I'm close to the edge again, my pussy throbbing from the pounding he's giving me. My clit is on fire. Connor watches and smiles, mouthing the word, "Come," at me.

I do. Screaming with pleasure, tightening around the turgid cock pumping into me. It sends David over the edge as well and he clutches on to my body as I buck beneath him. Our cries echo throughout the kitchen before the stillness sets in. He's draped over my body, his head near mine as we recover, breathing heavily. I look at him and he notices a few moments later, his expression back to the shy and embarrassed mix.

"Don't," I state plainly with a smile and he understands. He smiles in return and looks confident for a moment, despite the shy dip of his head away from me. Looking past him I see Connor has vanished from the window.

I lie on the counter as David tidies himself up. Propping up on my elbows, I watch him and wait for his next move. Once his pants are back on, he stares at me incredulously before ducking down for a tentative yet simmering kiss.

We pull apart and I break the silence.

"Thanks for the delivery." I quip with a smile, eliciting a laugh from him.

"Anytime," he responds and starts to move away. "I have to…" He trails off and I nod. He backs away, still staring at me until he bumps into the wall, and with an embarrassed wave, stumbles out the front door. I lie back on the counter and smile contentedly for a while before going back to uninteresting daily chores.

When I come downstairs later on, my landlady is pretending to dust the table in the foyer but stops as soon as I reach the last step.

"Your friend left this for you," she spat with a venomous tone as she handed me a small white envelope. *My friend?* I thought, curious as to whom she meant while hoping it was Connor. My watcher. I felt a tingle between my thighs as I opened the sealed envelope. Surprised she bothered to pass it along but even more so that she didn't take a peek, I smile thinking of how persuasive he could be, as I pulled the card out.

On a simple white piece of card stock he'd written:

Very good, girl. Tuesday. 8:00 p.m. Wear nothing. I'll be by.

I stared at the words and felt my legs go weak, my well-sated pussy throbbing as if it had not been touched in years. Looking up to thank my landlady for passing the note along, I found myself alone in the foyer. She must have slipped away while I was paralyzed by his words.

Turning to go back up to my apartment, I smiled and whispered aloud, "Yes, Sir."

A KEEPER

Sommer Marsden

W hat do you call this color?" John asked. He rolled the brownish, greenish, tanish paint onto the wall. His dark-blue shirt was dotted with paint. His surfer-boy blond hair was speckled with it, too. And his big chunky glasses were smeared with some more.

"Did you roll in it?" I laughed.

"Nope. I'm just a bit messy is all."

"The color is called, I-have-no-clue-it's-on-the-can. But I saw it in my cousin's clubbed basement and fell in love. It's one of those colors that changes with the light. One minute it looks green, then taupe, then silver...weird."

"Like you," he said, turning his back.

"I—what?" My throat grew a little tight. John was a bad-ass friend, a good guy, a fierce lover, but poor little me—burned by love one too many times—could not decide if he was a keeper. And yes, I say that poor little me with my tongue firmly planted in my cheek.

"Nothing." It wasn't a passive-aggressive kind of nothing, where he wanted me to coddle and pry and cajole. It was a straightforward, never mind—let it go—nothing. Another reason I liked this man. He was no drama and that was refreshing.

So many check marks in his favor and yet, I kept holding him at arm's length.

"Thanks for helping me paint," I said, suddenly shamed.

"No worries. You promised me some cold beer, your stellar company and pizza if I'm not mistaken."

"Fuck!" I pushed my hand into my hair and only caught myself when John chuckled. "I just smeared mystery-color paint in my hair didn't I?"

He grinned. It was a lupine grin that made me think of arousal tinted with danger, and my pussy went wet. It was swift and consuming—that flash of want. And it startled me.

"Don't worry, Starr, it works for you."

I stuck my tongue out at him and patted my pockets for my phone. No phone.

"Careful, don't stick that out unless you intend to use it," he teased.

There it was again. A lightning bolt of arousal searing me from my bones outward. I was losing my mind, or maybe I was coming to my senses. I found the house phone and dialed Dante's Pizza.

"I have an order for pick up..." I recited my usual order for when John came over. Two extra-large cheese pizzas, two fries, one salad—just for show.

I felt him take my wrist and squeeze, but the guy was talking. Giving me a total and a pick-up time. I heard the tape and paid it no mind. Do you know how much painter's tape I'd used in the last few days? It was only when blue tape kissed the thin skin at my wrists, that I turned to look. By then I was saying good-bye. John caught my other wrist before I could react and was swiftly taping my wrists together in front of my body. My instantly trembling body.

"What—?"

He plucked the phone from the crook of my neck and shoulder and put it down. "I just want to plead my case while we wait," he said. He kissed me and it was the boldest kiss he'd ever delivered. Warm lips and rough tongue and it shot right from my mouth to my cunt as I tried to process, smiling laughing John with intense and sexy John.

My John...

The thought was so pure and so instant I rejected it immediately. I would not be wooed into changing my stance. I wasn't ready. I wasn't able. I wasn't *suitable* to love or be loved. Not now. Maybe not ever.

And yet, when he unbuttoned my painting shirt—an old button-down that was speckled with a rainbow of paint colors—my nipples pebbled eagerly, begging to be touched. My stomach rolled with anxiety mixed with a brilliant excitement. We had fucked before, a lot, but something about this—about *now*—had me practically vibrating with urgency.

Whatever he was doing, whatever he wanted to do, the answer was yes. And it all stemmed from the look on his face. Cute and adorable had turned to sexy and wolfish. Dark-brown eyes seemed darker, smiling face now intent, relaxed brow now creased by focus. My hands were taped in front of me so he simply peeled back the halves of my shirt. When he gazed at me, I felt scrutinized and on display and my cunt flexed wetly at the emotion it caused. Joy.

"Your case?" I swallowed hard and tried to wrangle my mind into paying attention to his words and not the hypnotic way he was dragging the rough roll of tape down the very center of me. From my collarbone, past my navel, to the very top of my hip bone that was barely peeking from beneath my ratty old gym shorts.

"I think you have this...*idea of me.* And that man, the one in your head, is not worth you taking that risk you don't want to take."

"I'm not—"

"Ready for love, yeah, yeah," he said. "You know, right about now I could totally start singing some bad-ass eighties rock."

His half grin struck me in the solar plexus and a snort of unexpected laughter burst out of me. "Please don't."

"Okay." He leaned in and almost kissed me. But he didn't. He brought his lips so close to mine I could feel a tingle of imagined energy, but there was no kiss. At the last moment, he diverted from my mouth and latched on to my nipple. The heat from his tongue lit me up from the inside. A single suck had my insides pounding steadily with my runaway pulse.

He brought me down to a feral place in that one moment. I wanted him to fuck me. In fact, I'd passed wanted minutes before and had swiftly veered into needed. I *needed* John to fuck me.

"Now you may wonder why I have taped you up, pretty Starr. And the reason is, I think you need to see me for who I am. *All of it.*"

Why did that almost scare me? Why was there a flicker of unease in me? From the heavy hint of predatory glee in his voice? My heart wanted to be a tiny bit scared, but my body leapt to attention.

"Like what?"

"Like I am the nice guy who does nice things." As he spoke, he pushed my shorts down. I was as bare under them as I'd been under my buttondown. He grunted appreciatively when he saw me and that sound set off a rush of fluid between my thighs. That sound that said he liked what he saw made my craving for him worse. Much worse.

I shifted restlessly in place, rubbing my thighs together and finding no relief in the action.

"You are a nice guy," I agreed.

"But I think bad things sometimes," he said, slipping a finger between my nether lips. And here we were again, like with the kiss that wasn't a kiss. He was touching me but not. He'd slid that finger between my lips and had it rested over my clitoris. But he didn't press and he didn't rub. He just left it there, not moving, so that I had to fight the insane urge to move my body against his finger.

I refused.

I chewed my lip before saying, as calmly as possible, "Like what?"

"Like showing you how it displeases me that you don't consider me worth... *more*."

I swallowed again, feeling breathless.

"I'm—"

"Don't say you're sorry," he said, flexing that finger. But only once, just briefly.

Warmth flooded my pelvis and I sighed. It was so good—that small movement.

"But I am."

"I *am*," John said. "Worth more, I mean."

"Of course."

Something in his voice had me standing ramrod straight. My nipples were hard knots of traitorous flesh, signaling to him exactly how turned on I was. There was no denying that this version of John made me hot. And a bit nervous.

"So I'm displeased." He pinched one of those rudely pointing nipples hard enough to make me wince. It was just a shade too hard and that knowledge had me practically panting.

"I'm sorry." I said it anyway. We both knew by the way I said it that I meant I was sorry for his displeasure.

He circled me slowly, moving behind me so that his breath, as he spoke, whispered across my neck. I shivered and my open shirt fluttered around my breasts and belly, tickling me. I almost didn't register what he said.

"I think you need to be more sorry."

I didn't turn when I heard him move. I was nearly afraid to, not just because I might see what he was doing, but because I was afraid of more displeasure on his part. As insane as that sounded. I was a bit bewildered: we'd played in the bedroom, him bossing me...me bossing him, no one ever taking it too seriously, but something in this John...

My John...

Something about this whole thing was different. I rubbed my legs together and felt the slick moisture at the very tops of my thighs. In my mind, I had a brief fantasy of him rushing me from behind. Bending me over, looping one of his big paint-speckled arms beneath my waist and taking me that way. Fast and hard and yes, boys and girls, *rough*.

Again, I'd drifted off and almost didn't hear him. "What's a fair number for treating me like the invisible man?"

I turned my head to ask him what he meant and saw the stirrer he held. A tremor started in my stomach and worked its way down into my cunt. What I was feeling was a mystery emotion—it couldn't decide if it was exhilaration or terror.

"Why do you have that?"

"Oh, this? Remember this?"

It was the only stirrer they'd had when we'd picked up the

paint. The clerk had joked it was a stirrer on steroids. Actually it was meant for industrial cans and it was huge. At least two feet long and four times as thick as a normal stirrer, we'd taken it as a joke. But John—this new John—was holding it and it didn't look like a joke.

"I remember," I said past a dry tongue. But god help me, my pussy tightened greedily around nothing at all. I liked a bit of pain, real pain, not play pain. And I had never ever admitted it to John, because I didn't think he'd be around long enough to need to know, truth be told. But now, here we were.

"So, I'll ask you again, Starr. How many do you think is fair? Can you see me now?" He waggled that chunk of wood at me and grinned.

"I can," I said.

"Good. Now give me a number, or I'll choose."

I studied him. Same kind face, brown eyes, chunky glasses. Same pretty, wheat-colored hair; same broad shoulders, flat belly, long legs. Same low-slung jeans and worn-out tee and big hands and... He slid the stirrer along the terrain of one of my bare asscheeks and goose bumps studded my thighs. I shivered.

"Five," I said.

"Come on now. Five? That seems pretty light for a girl like you." He tapped me on the hip with the stirrer and each tap reinforced how hefty the stirrer was. John watched my face and moved to stand in front of me. Then he slowly slid the piece of wood between my thighs. Inserting it an inch at a time, but never ever coming near to where I wanted him. Where I needed him. My merrily thumping clit.

I sighed. "A girl like me?" I managed.

"A girl who likes pain—"

"I never—"

"You never told me because you figured I'd be gone soon," he whispered. One time, for just a heartbeat, he rapped the narrow side of the stirrer to my clitoris and I cried out. I was so far gone that one hard tap had put me in an odd head space. Nearly desperate, definitely humbled.

I bit my lip.

"But I could tell," he said, pulling the stirrer free and stroking my thigh with it. "I watched your eyes when things got a bit rough. And the way you sighed when I'd lay those little love bites on you."

I blushed. I was a whore for those little bites. The ones that left small purple marks on my breasts and my shoulders and my collarbone.

"And I'm not a fool, Starr. When a woman comes that hard after a too-sharp nibble at her skin, well...I can put two and two together. Plus..."

He smiled and there—ah, there—were those adorable dimples and the cartoon-character brown eyes and the small chuckle and god, he was such a *nice* guy until...well, until, apparently he wasn't.

"Plus what?" I dared to ask.

John stepped up close to me so that we were eye to eye, nose to nose, naked tits to broad sheathed chest.

"I can smell it on you."

That broke me, those words, and I whimpered, my eyed darting away from his intense stare.

"So you still say five?"

"Eight," I said.

"Your lucky number," John said. "And oddly enough my lucky number doubled." He winked and sat on the painting step stool. "Come on then."

I didn't have to ask. I staggered forward on numb feet and draped myself over his lap. His cock was hard against my chest, his breath warm on my nape. The first blow brought my head up. The feel of impersonal thick wood connecting with my living flesh. Pain flared brightly, fading to pressure before unfurling into a warm slinky pleasure. The second blow crisscrossed the first and I gasped. The X I imagined on my bare ass a blazing red tattoo in my mind.

The third blow hit the opposite cheek and right before delivering four, he slid the smooth wooden instrument along my spine, rucking my shirt up as he went.

I sank into that lulling drag of wood against skin and when I relaxed just a hair, he brought it down for number four.

"My lucky number four," John said. "Let's check our progress."

His fingers slipped between my legs, the very tips parting my nether lips. He made a point not to touch my thrumming clit in any way, but just having his fingers so close was blissfully unbearable. When two fingers dipped into my slippery opening, I arched up to meet him. I didn't care how shameless it was.

"I'd say this is a raging success."

The next four blows were cake. I saw the light at the end of the tunnel. And even though they sparked like tiny livewires along my tortured, flushed skin, I gritted my teeth and bared them all. When I was done, his hand dove into my long red hair and he twisted a clump into his hand.

"I'm impressed."

So was I but I said nothing. A few stray tears had leaked out of me and I trembled there, from the rush of adrenaline and endorphins, still draped over his legs.

"Come on up here."

On the way, I brushed my face against his lap, my flushed cheek riding the rigid erection he had tucked away inside his faded jeans.

"You can do that later," he said, turning me.

John brushed his thumb along my lower lip and whispered, "Trust me. I have big plans for this perfect mouth."

My tongue darted out to taste the salt on his skin and I stared at him. This new John.

"But?"

"But for now, I want more."

He slammed me to the one unpainted wall and my body jarred, but the impact made my insides shiver for him. He worked his buckle and I stood there watching, my bound wrists aching but I didn't care. When he kicked off his jeans and boxers and advanced on me, juices graced the tops of my thighs and my stomach went light.

"Please," I said, and that was all. I wasn't even sure it made sense, and I was beyond caring.

He slipped my bound hands around his neck and kissed me. His tongue stroked over mine and when I kissed him back, he sucked roughly at my tongue so I felt the resounding tug in my pussy. One big arm looped beneath my right knee and hiked my leg up, the motion parting me, opening me to him, and then he was driving into me. One long easy stroke, I was so fucking wet.

His mouth came down on my shoulder, teeth glancing across feverish skin. His cock filling me, his big body working me over so I felt slightly crumpled and completely boneless. An orgasm swelled toward me as the skin on my bottom throbbed from the paddling. I was so prepped to come it was as easy as breathing.

He rocked into me a bit harder, sliding his pretty white teeth along my collarbone. I held my breath, anticipating the bite that did not come. He pressed against me, pinning me fully and cutting off my air. It was almost impossible to breathe. And that's when his teeth really clamped down, the pain flashed bright and wonderful and I came, gasping for air that wasn't there.

He held me steady, not letting me move, and lost his manners. His thrusts an exercise in chaos, his hips rotating and driving, seeking nothing at that point but pleasure.

When he came, I kissed him fiercely. Sucking at his lips to lick that sound away. The sound of us fucking—for *real*—for the first time. The first time I was myself entirely. No walls, no fear, no hiding.

John took my face in his hands for just a second. Brushing his thumbs along my cheeks before he let me go.

"Now that I've expressed myself, you have a decision to make. I'm a nice guy but even nice guys get tired of waiting," he said, ripping the blue tape from my wrists. My skin rejoiced as if inhaling deeply. The blood flow brought pins and needles to my skin.

I just stared at him. Taking him in.

"Starr?"

"Yes. I heard. A nice guy."

"I am right?"

"Yes, you are. You're a nice guy, John. My John." I blurted it out, and when his eyes met mine I felt my cheeks color.

He gave a nod. "That's what I've been waiting to hear. Now we have pizzas to go get." He bent to grab his jeans.

I watched him move. Drinking him in with new eyes. Okay, so I'd been wrong. He was a keeper, after all.

BONDAGE BLOGGING

Meadow Parker

We were pretty deep into the evening when I realized that Jamie and Andre were planning on tying me up.

What finally tipped me off wasn't the hand massage Andre was giving me or the way that Jamie caressed the back of my neck; both of those seem obvious in retrospect, but at the time that wasn't what convinced me.

It was when Andre started asking questions about my sex life.

"I never did get to ask you if you play," said Andre, his chocolate eyes bright and his wide, gorgeous mouth twisted up in a grin. "Do you?"

His big, dark, powerful hands, which had been massaging my fingers and palm, moved up to my wrist. My other hand was limp on my thigh.

So this was how it was done, huh? This was how the bondage bloggers did it? Was that all it took to get a girl into bed? Two beers and a comment about carpal tunnel? "Here, I'll show you something that helps," he said, massaging my fingers. And then, with that grin that always melted me, he added: "If it works, I can teach it to your boyfriend."

And me, with my dorky little flirt in response: "If I *had* a boyfriend."

"Girlfriend?"

I said, *"No,"* a little too quickly, a little too loudly, and then added, "Never," a little too emphatically, which made me worry that Jamie might stop what she was doing to my neck.

She didn't. The gentle touch of her fingers, in fact, turned into something very close to a kiss, except there was no actual contact yet. Just the whisper of her breath and a ripple down my back to my butt, which suddenly felt all wicked and squirmy and tingly with the memory of just how pretty *her* butt looked when it was very red and very striped because Jamie was face-down, ass up, whipped, gagged and struggling.

She didn't kiss me, though—not yet. She just sort of leaned in and *breathed* on me.

I could feel myself responding. I got positively wiggly in my shorts. I felt dorky in them, and in my dumb South-By-Southwest T-shirt a size too small to begin with and washed on hot like all my clothes because I simply can't be bothered. I hadn't really dressed for seduction. But then...does anyone ever *really* dress for *being seduced*?

Maybe someone other than me, I guess. Having stewed all day in the ninety-degree heat and my airless hovel of a top-floor apartment, I had figured it would be dumb to dress to impress so I tried to look casual. My one kinky outfit had been purchased a week before and remained unworn, hanging in my closet, waiting the three days for Folsom. It was *not* safe for drinks with friends at Lombardi's on a weeknight, even if those friends were in fact Internet famous.

I had showered out of politeness, of course, and slathered on some makeup—I always do when meeting new people, though heaven knows why since I always end up feeling like I walked into Tammy Faye Baker at the mall. I usually call it quits when there's slightly more lipstick on my lips than my T-shirt.

It was a nice warm weeknight, and the patio was warm and calm and we mostly had it to ourselves. There were hyacinths, and the scent caressed my senses as gently as Andre and Jamie were caressing my neck and my hands and my wrists. The scent of the flowers gave me a little tickle deep inside. I felt high. So I answered Andre...sort of.

"Um," I said, "I don't think so."

Andre looked at me like I was crazy. Jamie laughed lightly.

"What is that supposed to mean?" she asked, her voice soft and musical, close to my ear. "You don't think so? Are you telling us to stop?"

"No, no, *no*," I said, my face reddening quickly. "I mean, about Andre's question. I don't think I've ever *played*."

Andre cocked his head, tossing his dreds in a rakish gesture. His grin just *melted* me.

"Well, if you don't know," he said, "who does?"

Now I was very red, and Jamie was laughing more lightly, which only made her breath feel warm and gentle and sexy on my neck. She brushed her lips there, and it felt like lightning ran through me. She kissed my shoulder and I felt her tongue—just a hint of it. I made a strangled noise as I tried to talk.

I stammered, "I've done a few things. But I've never done a *scene*. I mean, not really. This guy I was seeing—we tried, but...no, I don't think I've ever really done much."

"Well, what have you done?" asked Andre, leaning in a little closer as his hands caressed my forearms. There were gentle swells of pleasure coursing through my body; the farther up my arm he stroked, the farther down my arm Jamie kissed me. Now her tongue was shameless and active. Andre held my hand up so she could take it from him; her fingers laced through mine and she brought my arm back a little so she could kiss it wetly.

One of his hands traveled up to my face; he brushed my hair away and gently touched my ear.

"If you don't mind my asking," he said. "Or...we can stop. You're not uncomfortable, are you?"

I was *very* uncomfortable, but I *didn't* want them to stop. I was uncomfortable because I knew there wasn't a damn thing they could tie me to without getting the cops called.

This absolutely isn't happening, I told myself. It couldn't be. What would the kinky couple from The Secret Fire want with a boring little fan-girl like me? Free beer? They paid. To get shown around San Francisco? Survey says uh-uh. I live in Oakland, and I've only been here for a year and a half myself. I don't get out much. I haven't done much.

And now Andre was asking exactly what I *had* done...while his wife kissed my neck and he gently stroked my arm. It was helping my carpal tunnel, all right—which I don't even have.

So I answered Andre's question: *What have you done?*

I told them in detail—abbreviated detail, but it didn't really matter. There wasn't much to tell. Some scarves, some hand-cuffs, a boyfriend or two. At home, a pair of leather restraints, a dog collar and nipple clamps I used when I was alone. More stuff about when I was alone. Candle wax, clothespins, silicone cocks, a wire coat hanger—a hissing intake of horror at that. Ten lengths of premium rope mail-ordered from Phoenix, which I'd never taken out of the package because it scared and embarrassed me that I didn't know how to use it.

I didn't look Andre in the eye very much as I told the story, and Jamie was still behind me.

I didn't look him in the eye partially because when I did my tongue got thick in my mouth and I could barely speak, but also because I was embarrassed. But I wasn't embarrassed because my sex life was dirty. I got embarrassed because it was *lame*. I was twenty-six years old, for god's sake. How was this the most I'd done?

Andre smiled and listened. He sometimes asked questions. When he did, he asked them softly, gently, smiling; his questions were firmly respectful.

Jamie's questions *weren't*. She said very different things than her husband, in a very different tone of voice. She was slowly becoming harder, scarier, the Jamie I knew from a few scattered posts. I thought about girls trussed and moaning, tits and butts striped with red, their faces between her legs while Jamie pulled their hair. She alternately kissed and slapped them and they always hugged her at the end. I felt her lips against my ear and I shivered.

Where Andre only asked clarifying questions, Jamie asked leading ones. She asked me nasty things. "You wished he'd hit you harder, didn't you?" "Does it turn you on to have your hair pulled?" "How wet do you get when you torture your nipples?"

This last thing was said as she eased her fingers up my T-shirt and down my bra and felt them, hard and sensitive. The answer, in case you're wondering, was and is *very*.

When she wasn't tweaking my nipples, Jamie let her caresses turn into scratches, as her sharp red fingernails began to bite into the sensitive flesh of my belly and breasts. All the while, she kept kissing and licking my neck. Toward the end, I felt her *teeth*.

It took ten or fifteen minutes to relate my entire history with bondage. Like I said, there wasn't much to tell, but Jamie managed to make it sound like the prehistory of a slutty little fuckslave who was begging to be tied up and hurt.

By the time I was done, it wasn't just Jamie feeling me up. Andre's hands were up my shirt, too; if he hadn't had such a big, broad frame, we might have been kicked out of Lombardi's by then. I was pretty sure we were about to be. I just didn't care anymore.

His thumbs worked my nipples. Jamie bit my neck. Her fingernails firmly raked my scalp as she pulled my blonde hair.

"And if a hot couple were to come across the bay and try to seduce you?" sighed Jamie. "Would a horny bondage slut like you invite them home to your place?"

"In fact," said Andre, taking his right hand out of my shirt so he could glance at his wristwatch, "I think we just missed the last BART train back to our hotel." I could see the clock behind him; it was barely past midnight. There were lots of trains left, but I wasn't about to tell him that.

"So I have to invite you home," I blurted. "But I don't have a couch." Again with the giggles. I sounded stupid. I hoped no one had a recorder going.

"We'll figure out something," said Andre.

I know it seems, in retrospect, like I should have known Andre and Jamie were planning to seduce me. Why else would they have crossed the bay at ten o'clock on a weeknight because they happened to be in town for Folsom Street?

But like I said. I guess I couldn't believe a pair of mini-celebrities would be all over me like that. I mean…Jamie and Andre were *Internet famous*. Weren't they out of my league?

I knew all about Jamie and Andre's sex life and their bondage adventures; that was how I knew them. I'd been reading their bondage blog for years. The Secret Fire. It was up for a few months on some little blogging site, but somebody gave them shit for the content of the photos. They moved it to another host, then another; the URL never seemed to stay the same for very long. They got a *lot* of traffic, judging from the zillions of comments telling them how hot they were. An embarrassing number of them were mine.

They never charged for the blog or the photos; they never censored a thing. Except for their *faces*. They'd show Jamie's pussy with Andre's fist inside it; they'd show her flesh distended by ropes and striped by whips and canes and reddened by Andre's hand, but they wouldn't show their faces. The closest they'd come was to show Jamie's gorgeous mouth up close as she screamed in orgasm. But it was never from an angle where you could have picked her out of a lineup; fans like me would probably have recognized Jamie's uvula before we recognized her face.

I had thrilled to Jamie and Andre's antics for more than a year. I'd gotten seriously turned on to their deeply poetic locker-room stories. I'd gotten up close and personal with my own secret flames and my even more secret *parts* while looking at pictures of Jamie tied to the couple's bondage bed. Once or twice, they'd brought home another girl, but they never mentioned how they knew her—or how the seduction was accomplished.

I guessed that maybe I was in the process of finding that out.

When they tied up girls, things got nasty. Not because of Andre—because of Jamie. Andre was a sadist, but mostly he was a gentle, strong, powerful and loving bondage dominant. Jamie was a bitch. She was totally a bottom to Andre (in the bedroom, at least), but when she got her pretty little red-nailed hands on a female playmate, she was a sadist *par excellence*.

And not in a nice way.

In the photographs of tied-up bodies Jamie sometimes wore a hood or a mask, or was shot from the neck down. It didn't matter to me; it wasn't their faces that made me follow their filthy adventures with such fascination. The fact that they were both damned good-looking—which I'd just found out an hour before—was more of a surprise to me than anything else about them. They weren't movie-star gorgeous, but they would have been hot even if ropes *hadn't* been involved.

But it all ended maybe a year ago, when "Professional commitments require us to suspend the publication of The Secret Fire..." If you want to know what a geek I am, I *actually screamed* when I read it. I'd gotten a little obsessed with them, and thinking of living without those hot and sexy updates every few days...ugh! I sent them an email and told them so—the first email I'd ever sent a blogger. They answered and stayed in touch.

And luckily for me, I'd downloaded every last picture and cut-and-pasted the text of their two or three hundred posts into Textpad and saved them on my hard drive. I reread them; when I got an e-reader, I even figured out how to convert the text to an e-book file so I wouldn't have to bring my laptop to bed anymore. I even resized their pics and offloaded them to my phone, so I could double-fist it if I wanted...pics in one hand, text in the other.

So yeah, I was a little obsessive about them.

That was probably made worse by the fact that for the last year I'd been willfully celibate—or, at least, I'd been abstaining from relationships. Since Jamie's hot blog posts and photos had been my primary masturbation fodder since the death of The Secret Fire, and my primary sexual outlet was with myself... that means I'd spent the last year touching myself to a dead blog. Does that count as necrophilia?

Meanwhile, whatever bondage community I knew anything about seemed to forget that The Secret Fire had ever existed. Maybe their fifteen minutes of fame were over. Was it possible that in cosmopolitan San Francisco, I was their number-one fan?

Maybe so. When Andre emailed me that they were coming to San Francisco for Folsom Street Fair and did I want to get a drink, how could I say no?

These were Internet mini-celebrities. They were my idols. They'd stoked my own secret fire more times than I could count. I'd had orgasm after orgasm looking at pictures of Jamie's bound body.

Looked like it was time to pay them back.

I warned them right off that my apartment is pathetic. I don't have bondage equipment or a four-poster bed. It was pretty embarrassing. They would have been much happier playing at the house of the friend they were staying with in the Mission—hadn't they said he had an actual *dungeon*?

Jamie silenced me with her hand across my mouth, while Andre grabbed my wrists and held them tight in the small of my back.

She said, "If you think we can't tie a girl up without a formal dungeon, maybe you didn't get the point of our blog. And besides…" She took her hand off my mouth and drew it softly down my throat. She smiled. "If you turn out to be fun to play with, maybe you'll get an invitation to the dungeon. We're here until Monday, after all…."

I was still thinking, *Holy fuck, a real dungeon*? when Jamie's hand went tight against my throat, and she slapped my face. Heat coursed through me.

"You like that?" she asked.

I tried to nod, but she was holding me too tight. She got the picture. She slapped me again. My face got warm. She stuck her thumb in my mouth. I obediently sucked on it.

Jamie kissed me, and I practically fainted. There was something fucking *hot* about the way she kissed. I'd never been kissed by a girl before. Her tongue felt all supple. Her face was so smooth. This wasn't anything like the little scratchy feeling of kissing a guy. It was *hot*.

While Jamie kissed me on the mouth, Andre stooped low and began kissing my neck, right where Jamie had been kissing it before.

As he did, he reached around my body and started undoing my belt.

He got my belt open easily. My jeans were so baggy he didn't even need to unbutton them to get his hand down them and into my panties. I moaned softly as I felt one finger between my lips. He found my clit and caressed it roughly, his finger drawing circles. Jamie lifted my shirt and popped my tits out of my bra. She dug her fingernails into my nipples and smiled as I squirmed.

"Now," she said. "Where are those nipple clamps you talked about?"

The nipple clamps, like the dog collar and the leash and the ball gag and the leather restraints and the knife and the candles and the lighter and the clothespins, were in the bottom drawer of my nightstand. The three silicone dildos and the lube and the two plug-in vibrators and the three battery vibrators were all in the *top* drawer of my nightstand. In fact, there wasn't much in my nightstand *except* sex and bondage toys. I had the sex toys on top because for some reason it seemed like it would be slightly less humiliating if anyone ever stumbled across them. The logic doesn't really hold up, but I guess whim had become tradition.

Jamie went through my gear while Andre kissed me and played with my tits. He was an even better kisser than Jamie.

"Where's that rope you bragged about?"

"I wasn't bragging," I whined, a little flirtatiously, half of me not wanting her to think I was pretentious, half of me hoping she'd think I was—and take it out on me. "It's in the credenza over by the window."

She found it while Andre pulled my T-shirt over my head and unclasped my bra. He pulled my jeans down to my knees and then pushed me down onto the bed. I propped my arms behind me, sitting on the edge. The jeans came off over my lace-up boots; so did my panties.

I tried to tell them I hadn't trimmed or anything, but Jamie had gotten on the bed behind me, way up on her knees. She's a lot taller than me. She had a ball gag in her hand.

She stuffed it in my mouth and buckled it snugly around me as Andre came in tight against me and forced my legs open.

"No more talking from you," Jamie said, as Andre's fingers worked into me. "We'll find out everything we want to know about you." She put her lips to my cheek and laughed sadistically. "It'll be like a whole year's bondage blogging, crammed into the next hour."

Now she had ropes in her hands. She and Andre pulled and pushed me back onto the bed, and the whole time Andre was up inside me—his fingers, firm against my insides, with the heel of his hand on my clit.

I moaned into the ball gag as Jamie started tying me.

Just how they got me tied up so good, I have no idea. None of my boyfriends could ever manage it. I always figured you needed a four-poster bed. Not so, apparently.

The rope was perfect; Jamie and Andre cooed about it as

they traded off tying me up. They secured my wrists to my sides with a series of loops around my hips. They tied my tits up tightly with ropes going over my shoulders and down my back in a crisscross pattern. They put nipple clamps on me and buckled the dog collar around my throat. They hoisted me up—with Andre's hand still up inside me—and planted me arch-backed, legs spread, with Jamie cradling me. Andre secured my ankles to my hips and got down in between my legs, his tongue caressing my thighs.

He kissed my right thigh, then drew his big hand up and slapped my left one. He repeated the cycle, kissing and slapping. My thighs turned red fast, and he slapped me harder, sometimes five times in a row. I didn't have a whip, but he didn't need one. He hit me harder till my thighs felt hot and looked lobster red, and then he went back to kissing my thighs while Jamie lit a candle.

The candle flame burned hot above me; Jamie tried the wax on her hand, then gave an appreciative murmur. She lifted it high and dripped wax on my tits. I jerked as it struck me. It wasn't that hot; it had just surprised me a little. It's not as surprising when you're always the one dripping candle wax on your own tits.

Jamie made a disapproving sound. "You're not going to be a little wimp, are you?" she teased me. "That isn't *hot*. *This* is hot."

She brought the candle down low and more wax spilled out. It *hurt*. My tits really were more sensitive, tied as tightly as they were. I jerked again, arching my back. I moaned into the gag. Andre's mouth molded to my pussy and he started eating me out. His tongue worked up into my slit, but he took his time making his way to my clitoris; by the time he did, my tits were practically covered in candle wax, and Jamie had started on my stomach, putting her hand down to catch any that ran toward Andre's head.

I'd seen him eat Jamie out a hundred times in their video clips. The sight of it always made my thighs get weak. He was way better at it in person, and before long I was right up on the edge of an orgasm.

Andre knew it, too. He pulled back and put his hands on my knees and spread my legs wide. I was already bound, but he held me down as well—so Jamie could lower the candle to my thighs.

They were sensitive as hell—especially with how turned on I was. I spasmed all over with each drip. Jamie brought it closer. The wax got hotter. Andre's fingers worked up into my pussy again, but he went really slowly. He was teasing me. He kept on teasing me till my thighs were covered and I was just about crazy with need. Jamie had burned the candle halfway down at that point; wax covered my tits and my stomach and thighs. She didn't have much of me left to torture.

"You want my husband to fuck you? Or do you want to get off on one of your fun little toys?" She held up the biggest of my three dildos—and when I say *biggest*, I mean *biggest*. I'd never successfully got it inside me. (Though I *had* had a lot of fun trying.)

I looked at Andre and nodded. He unbuttoned his shirt and shrugged it off. There were condoms in the nightstand; Jamie found one and tossed it to him. He opened his pants, took out his cock and sheathed it.

Jamie leaned over me, reaching down to guide him in. He was big and hard and curved just right and really took his time teasing me, going slow at first while he looked in my eyes. Even so, he didn't have to fuck me very long before I was almost there.

But it didn't hurt that Jamie took her shirt off and leaned down to rub my clit as Andre fucked me.

I came like *crazy*.

Andre didn't rush through it after I'd climaxed hard on his cock. He let Jamie lean me back so he could look in my eyes, and Jamie cuddled up and looked at me with him. It would have been slightly creepy if I hadn't seen them a million times in my fantasies, doing things just as dirty as this, and maybe dirtier.

She took my nipple clamps off while he fucked me. I felt the pain explode through me, flying high on endorphins. She also untied the rope that held my ankles to my hips and forced my back up in an arch; it had made it *really* easy to come, but my back was aching.

With only my wrists tied, I could wrap my legs around him. Andre fucked me deeper with each stroke, his heavy, hard body atop me. He took his time, as he'd taken his time with every-thing. Jamie got completely naked at some point. She slid up against me and kissed my face and neck while her husband took his pleasure with my cunt. I'd never experienced a man going this long; he seemed to know exactly how to please himself, and please me while he was doing it. I guess he'd had a good teacher.

Jamie never stopped kissing and playing with me while Andre fucked me—and when she unbuckled my gag, we started making out. Andre leaned back with his knees tucked under my butt, sweat-covered and beautiful above me, watching the two of us kiss; he looked like he was in heaven.

When he finally let go, it was *gorgeous*.

Jamie caressed his broad back as he came, and kissed his neck...exactly like she'd kissed mine.

She helped him pull out with the condom intact.

Then they undid my ropes, and we all shared the bed.

I can't say it's easy to get a good night's sleep with three people in a full-size bed, when one of you is covered with solidified wax that keeps showing up in awkward places.

But then, we didn't really have sleep on our minds.

I got that hoped-for invitation to their friend's dungeon in the City, after all, but I didn't get much sleep there, either.

THE SATURDAY PET

N. T. Morley

As they left Bonne Femme, Luis said something to Tera that made her heart stop.

"Let's go to the pet store."

Neither Tera nor Luis had a pet.

Well, it could be said in one sense, that Luis *did* have a pet. It was not a canine or feline beast, however; his pet was Tera. He kept her and groomed her, dressed her when he saw fit and left her undressed when he saw fit to do that instead. For their trip to the mall, he had done something in between; she wore a bit of a dress, but not much else. Although Luis had just dropped hundreds of dollars on lingerie, none of what Tera already owned had made it onto her body before they left the house for the mall.

She had asked to wear a bra, but Luis wasn't having it. She'd even tried to get him to let her wear panties, which she usually didn't—certainly never on a Saturday, and never when the weather was so warm.

But Luis had said, no, just the dress and the heels, and there wasn't much to the former. The dress was quite a slutty little sundress, pale yellow and almost see-through, low-cut and short. Tera's body was revealed quite plainly at several key places—her pert little butt, her cleavage, her nipples. Between the way the dress plunged and the way the thin yellow cotton hung to her flesh, Tera felt almost more naked than if she'd been naked. She felt almost more revealed walking through the concourse at the mall than she had when she'd stripped down in the changing room and cycled through numerous skimpy lace outfits for Luis. By insisting that Tera wear a dress so thoroughly revealing to go to the mall to try on slutty lingerie, Luis had reminded her—as if she could ever forget!—that her body was his to show off, and that she need not worry about whether others wanted to look. If it pleased Luis to *let* them look, they would look. It was as simple as that.

And this was only one of the many ways in which Luis controlled her life—deliciously so. He decided when she would eat, when she would sleep. He told her when and in what way she would shower, and whether she would use the shower massager to bring herself off—or, much more commonly, to bring herself right to the edge and then back off. He decided when she would touch herself elsewhere, too. She did so in bed while he was at work, sometimes, when he gave her permission by phone—always with the proviso that she would have him on speakerphone when she did, and that she would ask permission before she came. Sometimes he gave it. Other times he did not. If permission was granted, Luis insisted that Tera come very loud for him. She never, ever failed him; Tera loved being a "screamer."

Tera was trained and usually obedient. Sometimes she did not obey her owner—and then she was punished.

How else could a pet be defined?

She might kid herself and identify as his "girlfriend," but she was a girlfriend who did exactly what he told her, when he told her. All that was required for her to be utterly subject to Luis's whim was for Tera to be in "that place"—meaning "sub space," as he called it. But the fact was that Tera was there in sub space with increasing frequency lately. And when she was not, she was ever aware that Luis could put her there with a stern look, a caress at her neck or a single harsh word. She almost never talked back to him anymore; she almost never needed to. She always wanted to do as he said.

More and more, Tera found herself her boyfriend's plaything.

And so Tera said, with only the slightest embarrassed quaver to her voice:

"Yes, darling...I think that would be lovely."

It was a glorious day and the mall through which they walked was a vast suburban structure, its skylights open to the outside and sunbeams streaming beautifully down. Tera felt largely neutral toward the existence of this mall, though very positive toward the fact that it was the only place around to shop for lingerie. She liked the fact that Bonne Femme, the expensive "intimates boutique," had a big enough and private enough dressing room that Luis could be admitted to sit with her while she tried on lingerie for him.

Tera knew from experience—she often slipped away and went there in the middle of the day when Luis was at work—that for most women, the companions who came into the fitting room to give opinions were more often girlfriends. Perhaps it was a little scandalous in this drab suburb that Luis was often there with her as she tried on a whole parade of sweet nothings.

But the store clerks did not know that Luis insisted on snapping photos of each outfit on his cell phone as Tera tried it on. "So I can recall what worked and what didn't," he said. "For when I'm deciding what you'll wear to bed."

Luis *always* decided what she'd wear at night. It aroused Tera intensely to put on exactly the lingerie he specified, in exactly the way he ordered. Almost as much as it turned her on to try it on for him.

In the end, he'd bought her several new garter belts, a cute little bustier, a white rhinestone-studded merry widow, a corset, and three cute see-through nighties. They were all very slutty—extremely suggestive. Tera had very much enjoyed looking at herself in the full-length mirror while Luis sat there, wearing his suit even though it was Saturday—the son of a bitch always wore a suit.

Occasionally, when Tera was "between outfits"—meaning she was stark naked except for her high-heeled shoes—Luis would finger her a little, just to keep things interesting.

If the ladies who worked at the shop thought something dirty was going on in the fitting room, they didn't say a word.

At least, not to the couple. Perhaps the clerks knew they could count on a very large sale. Or perhaps they wished to save their gossipy comments for each other, after Tera and Luis had left. Regardless, they left with their arms full of packages—hundreds of dollars' worth of pet wear for Luis's favorite pet. Only one thing remained.

"Let's buy you a collar," purred Luis softly, as he guided his excited girlfriend toward Pet Parade.

Tera had been in enough pet stores throughout her life. She and her family had both cats and dogs growing up, her older sister had a parakeet and her younger sister had hamsters. She knew all too well the strange mélange of scents that spelled "pet store" to anyone who'd ever visited one. It was a mix of cat food, dog food, birdseed, cat litter, rabbit shavings, plastic, leather....

It had never aroused her before. Now it did; it turned her on intensely. The great wall of collars loomed at the far end of the shop, and her heart pounded as she thought about one of those going around her throat.

Though the location of the collars was obvious from where they both stood at the front of the store, Luis saw fit to engage the pretty clerk—packed into a tight yellow polo shirt and snug jeans—in their charade.

He asked as soon as they walked in: "Where would I find the collars?"

He looked Tera up and down before he added, "For a dog about one-oh-five."

Tera's thighs felt like rubber. She reddened. Luis made a soft, sharp clicking sound as he walked with his walking stick behind the helpful female clerk, making no attempt to camouflage the open interest he felt toward her butt as she led the way. Tera had to admit it was a very nice butt. She wondered if the clerk had ever worn a collar.

Luis thanked the clerk, who told them to summon her if they had any further questions. If she knew why the collar was being bought, she played it reasonably cool—but that was more than just a typical flirty smile Tera glimpsed on the clerk's face as she flitted away back to the counter.

Luis reached up and withdrew the first collar from the wall. It was big and black leather and had shiny metal studs on it.

He set their lingerie bags aside, leaned his walking stick up against a shelf and held the collar up to Tera's throat.

Tera recoiled. "You're not going to put that thing on me, are you?" she hissed. "In public?"

Luis answered: "Of course I am."

"But people are watching!" said Tera, her face now very red. She felt a fierce and powerful arousal as humiliation washed through her.

"How else," Luis asked, "do you propose I ensure a proper fitting for my pet?"

Tera gulped and said, "But it's not *supposed* to fit *me*!"

"Says who?" smiled Luis, his voice a soothing purr. "It's for a *pet*. And as you'll recall, it's my decision who knows you're my pet. Isn't that what I told you when I made you lift your skirt for that trucker last weekend?"

Tera blushed very red; her nipples stood out painfully through the thin cotton dress. She'd forgotten all about that. Her clit throbbed. Her pussy felt wet; her thighs seemed slick, and it wasn't just from sweat. The air-conditioning of the pet store chilled her flesh.

"Yes, Sir," she said.

"And he liked it quite a bit, didn't he?"

"Yes, Sir," she said.

"But I think you liked it more."

Tera nodded. "Yes, Sir."

"Then come here," said Luis firmly, "and let me fit my pet for its collar."

Tera felt dizzy. *It*. She was "It."

When Tera shied away again as he went to put the collar on her, he spoke very sharply to her.

"Tera, I won't ask you again. If I have to tell you again, that skirt is coming up...and that clerk who's been watching us so intently is going to see you get your ass reddened."

The second he mentioned spanking her, Tera was helpless to resist. She already knew she could expect to be spanked when they got home—just for questioning Luis's order. But she was positively destroyed by the thought of having it happen right here in the pet store. She knew she'd be revisiting that hope-fully-never-to-happen moment in her fantasies the next time Luis gave her permission to masturbate.

Tera stepped forward; Luis buckled the collar around her throat.

If the clerk at the counter had not known before what—or whom—the collar was for, she certainly knew now. She was watching them like a hawk.

And from the look on her face, she certainly seemed to approve. The pretty young woman could not have been much older than twenty, but she clearly knew her way in the world.

Luis tugged at the heavy D-ring of the black leather collar. Its weight sent a ripple through Tera's body.

"This one will do for when you're at home, fighting my authority...like you just did. But I think you need a prettier one for when you're out in public. One that matches that rhinestone merry widow I just bought you...don't you think?"

Tera's eyes went wide. Her jaw dropped. Her mouth twisted in an expression of horror. "In...in public?" she whimpered.

Luis planted his mouth on hers and kissed her deeply.

As he kissed her, he tugged at the D-ring of the heavy leather collar. The pressure on the back of Tera's neck sent a spasm of pleasure through her.

Luis took the black leather collar off her and set it aside.

He took down a far more slender collar—one of white leather, with rhinestones circling it. It had a delicate little buckle. There was no D-ring on it; it was clearly not made for a leash. And it was made for a female dog...one about Tera's size. It must have been made for a very large dog who *always* followed its master's commands.

Tera felt the snug embrace of the smaller collar as Luis

buckled it around her throat. Tera saw his eyes widen. He seemed to catch his breath.

"What a shame," he said, "that they don't have mirrors in pet stores. You look quite stunning in it. Once I get you in that rhinestone number..."

Tera frowned. The white rhinestone-studded merry widow that Luis had just purchased for her had been bought over Tera's objections. She felt it made her look tacky, slutty and cheap. "I look like a stripper," she said. "I don't want to look like a stripper!"

"But that's not for you to decide," Luis had told her.

"This one doesn't have a D-ring for a leash," he said breathlessly. "It's only for when you're very, very good. For when I know you'll do exactly as I say. When no leash is necessary. Can you promise me you'll try to earn this collar, Tera? Otherwise..."

With a smile, Luis reached up and seized a leather leash from the wall—a huge, long one with a big leather loop and a chain at the end; the clip that hooked to a beast's collar was clearly made to resist the pull of a very strong dog.

He held up the black leather leash and the black leather collar together, and said firmly, "Try to earn the pretty little one, will you? Try and be a good pet for me?"

Tera nodded emphatically. Her voice rich with arousal, she whimpered, "Yes, Sir. I'll try."

He took the rhinestone collar off of her. They gathered the Bonne Femme bags, the leash and the two collars.

They took them up to the clerk, who rang them up.

Her eyes lingered lushly in a slow circuit from Luis to Tera, then to the collars.

She named their price.

Luis winked at her.

The young pretty clerk blushed. She was forced, by the pet store chain, to wear a uniform polo shirt that was not very flattering to her figure. She chose, however, to wear it two sizes too small. The strained fabric tented slightly more as her nipples stiffened.

Both Luis and Tera could see this happening as the clerk ran Luis's credit card, and he signed.

Tera and Luis left the pet store.

Outside, right where the clerk could see them...right where *anybody* could see them, Luis stopped and opened the bag from the pet store.

"I think we know what kind of a collar you need for tonight, don't we?"

Tera didn't, but she answered, "Yes, of course, Sir." She hoped he would tell her, not ask her...because she didn't know if tonight Luis expected that she would be his obedient pet, pretty and perfect and cuddly—or a ravenous beast that needed to be collared and chained. Right now, she felt more like a beast. Her pussy ached to be filled. With Luis deliciously humiliating her in public like this, Tera didn't entirely trust herself not to throw herself on him in the car...or worse, try to wrestle him onto one of the mall's many benches and ride him like a pony before he could stop her. She was so turned on she feared she could not control herself.

She felt very much like an animal and wanted to be collared.

To her relief, however, Luis had more faith in Tera than she had in herself. He believed her to be a very safe pet.

He said: "You've been very good—even with all those people watching."

"They're still watching, Sir," gulped Tera nervously, shifting her body and wriggling from side to side as her deep sense of humiliated arousal only grew with her anticipation.

Luis smiled.

"Yes, there are quite a few people around, aren't there? Perhaps they'll know why a boyfriend would collar his girlfriend like this. Perhaps they'll know what this means."

He reached into the bag and took out the white rhinestone collar. He held it up. He fished his penknife out of the pocket of his suit pants and sliced the tag off the collar.

Tera made surreptitious glances all up and down the mall. There were people standing nearby and a few were watching them—a group of college girls, a trio of food-court employees who seemed to have just gotten off work. Tera felt very aroused and very embarrassed.

Luis held up the collar for her.

He said, "I won't need leash tonight, will I? Will you do everything I say tonight, Tera? Will you be my very good pet?"

Tera nodded and stepped forward into the embrace of the white rhinestone collar.

She felt Luis buckling it around her throat. She never looked away as he did so, and neither did he; they locked eyes until the white rhinestone collar was secure around her throat.

"Yes," she told him. "Everything."

His arms went around her. He held her close. His body felt warm as his hands came to rest on her ass.

He turned her around and steered her toward the parking lot.

WILDERNESS TEST

Veronica Wilde

Karenna didn't know whose cock was pushing inside her, but she knew it felt good. Her thighs ached wider, though they were already chained apart to the legs of the cot. When the man withdrew, she moaned in frustration. A single fingertip teasing her clit was the only response and then, as she whimpered in complaint again, low male laughter.

"You really get off on this, don't you?" Tim asked.

Karenna scowled. "Dammit, Tim, I told you not to talk! Now you ruined it."

He lifted her blindfold, peered into her green eyes and kissed her. "Sorry. You just looked so hot."

He tweaked her nipples, sighing lustfully over her full, naked breasts. Then he drove all seven inches of his cock inside her. Though he hadn't tugged her blindfold back down, it felt good. Karenna closed her eyes and returned to the fantasy that she was being taken anonymously by some sexy brute who'd tied her up.

It was hard to steal these moments alone at the summer camp where they both worked as junior counselors. They slept in separate cabins shared with other counselors and sneaking off into the woods for a quick fuck just wasn't easy with so many young campers wandering around. Right now they were supposed to be down at the lake for the daily afternoon sailing/swimming session—but they had bribed other junior counselors into covering for them.

Something rustled in the greenery outside. Karenna peeked out. Tim was moaning on top of her, oblivious, but there was a silhouette outside the open cabin window behind him, a male outline with the sun to his back. Excitement flooded her face. Just like in her naughtiest fantasies, a man was watching her get fucked while she was tied up and naked. A man who clearly liked watching her breasts bounce, her pussy speared by Tim's thrusting cock.

A dizzying whirlpool of heat began in her pussy. She was going to come and soon. She grunted, arching her back and imagining who it could be. Probably it was one of Tim's friends leering at her but oh, how badly she wanted it to be one of the hot senior counselors. Older and remote, too cool to associate with their younger colleagues, the senior camp counselors were way sexier than her fellow junior counselors like Tim. Especially Dax, the darkly sexy and hard-muscled leader, with his deep tan and slow, dirty smiles.

"God, your pussy feels so good..." Tim was fucking her into a frenzy. A primitive cry tore from Karenna's throat as her cunt closed around him, squeezing him in wet, blissful throbs.

That night, after the official lights-out saw the campers safely in their beds, Karenna and the other junior counselors gathered for their nightly campfire. This was her favorite part of the day, when they could crack open a cold beer and laugh under the stars.

This was her first summer working at this camp. She hadn't been too wild about the idea, but once she got here, she saw the advantages of spending four weeks at a campground where no one knew her. Here she might be able to live out her secret fantasies of bondage and submission—all the things she was too shy to request back on campus from her college boyfriends. It seemed safer here to experiment. She'd quickly seduced Tim with an eye to shaping him into the dirty, dominant man of her dreams. Whenever they found an hour to sneak off into an empty cabin, Tim tied her up and bossed her around just as she directed. But though the sex was good, it didn't quite hit all those forbidden, degrading notes she craved.

Her mind returned again to the senior camp counselors. The junior counselors were in college, but the senior counselors were all well into their twenties. They were in charge of actually running the camp, from the dining hall to the sailboats. Karenna dreamed of submitting to one of them, especially the coolly aloof Dax, who was so curt and unattainable.

"I heard something," said another counselor uneasily. She looked over her shoulder at the woods. While they were allowed to have campfires, most of them were under drinking age and the senior counselors had warned them that alcohol wasn't allowed.

"Raccoon," Tim dismissed. He held out a hand. "Smitty, throw me another one."

"Actually," said a deep voice, "why don't you throw us one, *Smitty.*"

Three of the senior counselors walked out of the woods. Everyone groaned with disappointment, but Karenna's first thought was of how tanned and glowing Dax looked in the firelight. His dark brows knit over almond-shaped eyes and his rumpled dark hair fell over his forehead.

"You really thought we wouldn't bust you?" another senior counselor asked. "You've been told time and again there's no alcohol allowed for junior counselors."

They ambled to the cooler and helped themselves to the remaining beers. "You all need to go back to your cabins," Dax ordered. "We'll deal with you tomorrow."

His eyes flickered over Karenna. Her nipples stiffened. Was it her imagination or had he directed that at her? Again she remembered that shadow at the window watching Tim fuck her. Maybe it had been Dax, checking to make sure none of the junior counselors were skipping out on swimming/sailing. A low, warm arousal loosened in her body.

The junior counselors got to their feet and began the walk back to their cabins, grumbling about losing their beer. But Karenna couldn't stop wondering what tomorrow would hold.

The next day each of the junior counselors received notes informing them of their scheduled meeting with a senior counselor. Karenna smirked to see that she was meeting privately with Dax, just after dinner. She already knew from Tim and the other junior counselors what their punishments were—a ban on campfires for a week. "It's goddamned ridiculous," Tim grumbled. "You think they weren't drinking when they were junior counselors?"

Karenna was so nervous she could barely eat a bite at dinner. Afterward she ran to change into her sexiest shorts, along with a white cotton camisole that showed off her full, round breasts. After brushing out her long hair, she walked down to the campground office where Dax was waiting.

He was leaning over the desk, reviewing reports. His dark

gaze lifted disdainfully. "Shut the door. Stand over here, in front of me."

She obeyed. She felt even more nervous standing next to him, his tanned face level with her crotch. "Word has it, you didn't attend swimming/sailing yesterday. Is that true?"

"I—" She tried to think of a way out of this. "You're right. I didn't. It was just the one time."

"That's a much more serious infraction than the beer last night. So your punishment will be a little different."

Now his dark, implacable eyes met hers. She knew that he'd been the one watching her get fucked yesterday. That—just maybe—he'd even raided their campfire last night deliberately to set up this punishment.

"Punish me however you see fit," she said. Her voice was trembling and, god help her, her panties were soaked. "I'll do anything you tell me to."

A cruel smirk played around his lips. Almost as if to say, *it's not going to be that easy, kid.* "I'm not even sure why you have a job here," he went on. "You're supposed to be teaching the campers how to sail, how to identify plants in the woods, how to become strong and self-reliant. Instead you're slipping off with your boyfriend."

"I'm sorry." She meant it, too. Dax vibrated with a dark, menacing energy.

"Are you listening?"

"Yes, yes!"

He stood up, all six feet of him looming over her. "Then let's get going. You have a wilderness test to pass."

He led her down toward the marina, where the sailboats glowed in the deepening dusk. No one was down here at this hour and she fantasized briefly that he would push her into the marina office and rip off her camisole. She couldn't take her eyes from his hard thighs. Instead he led her past the boats and up a dirt path into a part of woods the campers weren't allowed to enter.

He stopped her and pulled out a black blindfold. "First test," he said casually. "Your tracking skills. Right now you're not going to see where we go, but later I'll expect you to trace the same trail."

Ridiculous. There was no requirement for junior counselors to be expert trackers. "Okay..." She swallowed as his amber eyes met hers. He slid the blindfold over her eyes. Just like that, the world went dark.

"How...?" How was she supposed to follow him blindfolded? But Dax lifted her wrists and began tying them together.

Oh, god. This really was going exactly where she'd hoped.

"What kind of a knot is that?" he asked. "You're supposed to teach the different knots used in sailing—what one did I just use on you?"

"I have no idea," she protested.

Dax snorted and yanked the rope, tugging her forward. She followed behind him closely, a leashed pet, bumping into him on occasion. She could tell from the rising insect choir that night was falling in the woods and her vulnerability made her feel scared and horny and excited. Then Dax stopped her again. He pressed something into her hands—a plant.

"What is that?" he asked. "Junior counselors should be able to identify the plant life of the woods."

She groaned. "I have no idea, but it better not be poison ivy."

She knew immediately she hadn't been deferential enough. Dax yanked on the rope. "Okay," he said. "I knew you were a disobedient counselor, but I had no idea you'd need this much discipline. You are going to be retrained, starting now. Lesson one: obey your senior counselor."

Suddenly her tied wrists were rising over her head. Dax was

tying her to something overhead, probably a tree branch. She blushed at the way this position thrust out her breasts.

"Now," he said, circling her, "as your senior counselor, when I tell you to do something, you do something. Without question. Understand?"

She nodded breathlessly. He moved her long hair over her shoulders. "Now," he said. "I want you to tell me exactly what you were doing yesterday during sailing/swimming."

She gulped. "I...I was with Tim."

"Tim? That skinny kid?" The contempt was clear in his voice. "And what were you doing with Tim?"

"I was...having sex."

"What kind of sex? I need a full confession. Start at the beginning."

Oh, god. Her pussy was so, so wet. All she wanted was for Dax to unzip her shorts and drive his thick cock inside her. It wouldn't take long, just a few thrusts, before she would come squealing and throbbing. But she could tell she was going to have to earn her orgasm.

"He...kissed me. And then he took off my top."

"Like this?" Dax unbuttoned her skimpy white camisole and roughly tugged it off, freeing her bare breasts. Never had they felt as full or hot or aching as they did right now. He cupped them, bouncing them in his hands. "And then what?"

"I...let him play with my titties." She could barely breathe as Dax stroked her nipples. "It felt really good."

"Keep going. Then what did he do?"

Her cheeks burned hot. "He took off my shorts...and I stood on the bed and spread my legs while he licked my pussy."

"You little slut." Dax sounded amused. "So that's what you do with the junior counselors. Strip naked and let them use you. I bet you show your pussy to lots of guys, don't you?"

She nodded wordlessly. A moment later he was unbuttoning her shorts and sliding them down her legs. "Well. Let's see what you're showing every guy in camp."

She was naked now in the woods, naked and blindfolded and tied to a tree, her entire body on display. Dax opened her legs and felt her pussy, tickling her for just a moment before circling her and cupping her ass.

He stepped away. She wanted to scream, beg him to keep touching her. "Then what?"

"Then he tied me to the bed and…" She swallowed. "He fucked me."

"Really? You barely know Tim. You always let guys tie you up and fuck you?"

One fingertip massaged her clit. Her body flushed with the embarrassing need to come. But the finger retreated.

Goddamn him! Why was Dax being such a tease?

"Well," he said. His voice sounded more distant, as if he'd stepped back. "Now we know the story. Skipping out on sailing/swimming to let some guy tie you up and fuck you. What do you think, Josh?"

Josh? What the hell?

"I think she's a horny little slut," drawled a Southern accent. Her nipples tingled. That was indeed Josh, the tall blond guy who coached the camp basketball tournaments.

"I think she's dying for our cocks," said a deep voice. Whoa. She had no idea who *he* was, and her body went electric at the idea of being fucked by a faceless stranger.

Dax lightly slapped her breasts. "Well," he said. "I think I have an idea of punishment."

She held her breath. All three of them fucking her, taking advantage of her tied up and naked in the woods. It was everything she'd ever fantasized about.

"And I think...scrubbing the dining hall floor every day ought to do it."

"No!" she begged. "Please, you can't leave me like this!"

"We can do whatever we want. But if you want a different punishment, you'd better beg for it right now."

"Fuck me," she whispered. "All of you. Do whatever you want to me."

Dax, Josh and the mystery man didn't say a word. She thought for a wild moment they'd walked off and left her. Then she heard a zipper, the muffled sounds of undressing. And what sounded like the rip of a condom wrapper.

Strong arms gripped her waist and pulled her forward. That thrilling hardness pressed between her legs, followed by a snicker—yes, it was Dax, and he was amused at how wet she was. Before she had time to feel humiliated, his cock pushed into her, splitting her open and filling her pussy. She groaned with helpless gratitude.

A low sound of appreciation came from the other guys. "Move to the side so I can watch her tits," suggested the mystery man.

Dax was gripping her ass now, mauling her body with rough hunger as he thrust in and out of her. He was grunting in time with his thrusts, driving into her with such energy that her bound wrists twisted wildly.

His body slapped hers with the rhythmic ferocity of her dreams. She was so dizzy with lust that she didn't hear the man moving behind her. His warm body pressed against her back, rubbing his hard dick on her ass.

"I love a soft juicy ass," he muttered in her ear. His teeth grazed her neck, sending a shiver down her spine. Then he parted her cheeks and stroked the tip of his cock between them, pressing gently against her asshole.

Karenna moaned her invitation. She loved anal sex, but she'd never been double-penetrated before and now it seemed that she was about to enjoy two stiff cocks fucking her for the first time. The man behind her—she didn't know if it was Josh or the mystery guy—worked his prick slowly into her asshole, barely moving as Dax rode her pussy with such force that he pushed her ass onto the other penis. Karenna bit her lip as the mystery man gradually lodged his shaft inside her. Being fucked by two men felt better than she'd ever imagined. A howl of pure joy escaped her, rising through the trees as the man behind her cupped her breasts.

"Oh, fuck," Dax breathed, humping her with strong, thorough thrusts. He went still, hissing between his teeth, and then withdrew from her with a sigh of satisfaction.

The remaining man stepped up and fondled her pussy. "So wet," he taunted. Yep, that was Josh. She could never face him at the basketball tournaments again, knowing how he would smirk at her. But he was pushing inside her, grunting with satisfaction, and all she cared about was getting fucked.

Both men were riding her in a seesaw rhythm, using her body like a soft and voluptuous plaything. Her breasts ached and her muscles were taut with excitement. A camera clicked; the knowledge that they were going to share these pictures with the other senior counselors, that all of them would jerk off to her bound and naked body, filled her with almost searing arousal, and her pussy began squeezing in a white-hot orgasm, gushing around Josh's cock.

He laughed softly. "You love this," he said mockingly. He pulled out of her and so did the mystery man behind her, and then all three of the guys were around her, fondling her pussy and playing with her breasts. She wasn't sure who was, because someone else was pushing inside her cunt again, another man in her ass. She swallowed, grateful to be getting fucked again because her body was still humming with tension and she knew she needed to come a second time, maybe even a third. She couldn't keep track of the cocks sliding in and out of her, the fingers squeezing her ass and groping her breasts. She was being fucked and bounced into a mindless, twisting vortex of animal pleasure. All too soon, a storm broke inside her, and she was coming again with a howl.

"That's right," someone grunted. He pulled her against him and groaned, his own orgasm pulsing inside her.

A sharp slice was followed by sudden freedom. They'd cut the rope from the tree. Her body slumped into someone's arms and they laid her on the ground. She didn't know if they were done with her, if more guys would arrive or if they had some new dastardly plan.

Someone moved her bound wrists over her head then straddled her chest, playing with her tits. She waited for his voice, for some clue as to who it was, but he said nothing. Then he lightly slapped her mouth. She opened her lips and the salty taste of his cock filled her tongue. He groaned softly and began to fuck her mouth, riding her face in a steady rhythm. She sucked him as best as she could, opening her legs in invitation to the other two. Someone knelt between her thighs, audibly rolling on a condom; the push of his cock followed a moment later. She twisted beneath the two men in mindless pleasure as they used her mouth and cunt.

The man fucking her face suddenly stiffened and gasped, a creamy spurt of cum filling her tongue, and he climbed off. To her surprise, the other man pulled out of her as well. They moved her onto her knees, tied hands in front of her. She guessed from this position that they weren't done with her mouth yet and sure enough, one of them stepped in front of her and thrust his erection into her mouth. She licked and sucked his cock as he played idly with her pussy. Goddammit. Were they really going to get her this excited without satisfying her? She wasn't sure who had come and when, but she knew they would get tired eventually. Maybe they would put her on all fours and one of them could fuck her from behind. She wiggled her ass as a hint but they just laughed and then the man in her mouth was coming with a long sigh of satisfaction.

She barely had time to swallow before another man replaced him. Something in the hard-muscled thickness of his body thrusting against her chest made her think it was Dax. His big cock filled her mouth and as she sucked his swollen crown, he reached between her legs and began to play with her, tickling her clit until she moaned. Excitement was rising higher in her like a hot flood. Dax groaned and pulled out of her mouth. She could hear him stroking his own cock as his fingers worked into her pussy, stroking her wetness in exactly the right spot. They came together, Dax shooting streams of warm cum all over her face as her own ejaculate streamed down her thighs.

She fell onto her side, shaking and still bound. Then her hands were lifted and with another slice, the rope was cut.

Finally. Her hands were shaking too hard to function properly at first but she pushed desperately at the blindfold, moving it from her eyes.

They were gone. Like forest demons, they'd melted back into the dark woods. She was alone, covered in cum and sweat and dirt.

Karenna caught her breath. She was almost too shaky to walk but she found her clothes, now damp with the evening dew, and then the path Dax had used to get here. She followed it down to the lake and slipped gratefully into the water, feeling clean and reborn. Surfacing, she looked up at the summer moon and listened to the noises of the night woods, unable to stop grinning.

BE THERE WITH BELLS ON

Joan Defers

S he kept her breath shallow, her movement fluid. Her hips swayed at half rate.

"A little faster," he murmured. "We don't have all day." She tried to ignore the impatient tapping of the crop against his knee.

She glanced down at the clamps. He'd attached small weights to chains, and dainty silver bells dangled from the ends.

She glided with the posture of a debutante fresh from charm school. She channeled ballerina. She was grace, poetry in motion, the stillness at the depths of a bodhisattva.

She transcended.

He wanted the glass dildo with blood-red and mint-green swirls, and he wanted her to retrieve it without producing even a single tinkle from those bells.

She took a few more steps. Why did the bathroom have to be so far away?

She bit her lip and blew out her tension slowly, relaxing her back muscles. Blood rushed to her pussy, and her thighs throbbed.

Oh, why did this have to affect her this way? Her nipples in the clamps, the cold chain draped between them. That's all it took to get her going anymore. She was easy, anymore. He was arrogant with it.

Her ears burned.

If she failed, so what?

He'd take that crop to her. He'd tie her up.

All things she enjoyed.

Even if she lost, she won. No need for panic.

She savored the challenge, giving in to an irrational need to prove to him that she was capable. The very act of demanding this useless, pointless task sent a jolt of excitement racing to her clit. The tightrope walk only made her ache with desire.

She reached the doorway and paused.

"Move it."

She stayed put another moment, feeling the weights sway.

He could, he had the option, he just might use that damned cane.

She hadn't ruled it out.

Of course, she hoped caning was reserved for a more egregious sin than the jaunty peal of a bell from a breast.

But the option never left her consciousness. It always hung in the air.

"I'm waiting," he said. "I don't want to wait."

"Yes, Sir."

She moved, even picked up the pace, ever so slightly. If only she had perfect little teacup tits, instead of her D-cup cliff. There was too much clearance, too much momentum.

Of course, if they just lay on her belly, where was the risk? He wanted the damned things swinging, threatening her with failure.

That was part of the fun.

He'd sent a text that afternoon, ordering her to make prepa-
rations. She'd carefully cleaned her little collection of toys, and
then laid them out on a towel, so they could dry in the bottom
of her bathtub.

And, he just had to have the Christmas dildo.

She misstepped on the rug in front of her sink, froze and
cringed, waiting for peal.

The bells didn't ring out, though. They just dangled, weights
tugging just perceptibly once more. Her cunt tingled.

She breathed again.

Damn it.

She released the tension in her shoulders, relaxed her abdomen
and continued her journey.

She breathed. She stepped.

"Almost there," he taunted, in that singsong tone he used to
tease her. His tapping grew more urgent, the tempo increasing.

She had a sudden impulse to just let the bells ring out. Rile
him up. Wipe that smirk off his face for just a minute, and refuse
him the satisfaction of her very best effort. He'd take her there,
in the bathroom, where things weren't so well lit or comfortable. Bad lighting, metallic echoes, all somewhat removed from
whatever ridiculous notions he held about the romance of her
overpriced apartment.

No silk sheets. No antiques. No playing pretend at Lord of
the Manor.

She could ruin this nasty little game of his.

She had, maybe, three steps to go. She was wet, loosened; she
felt every last movement, as the clamps jiggled.

She stopped at the bathtub's rim, and looked back at him, her
braid falling behind her right shoulder. He reclined on her chaise
lounge, his boots carelessly propped upon her upholstery.

Bastard. She'd paid sixty dollars a yard for that brocade.

He motioned her on with the crop. "Go ahead."

She delayed a moment, ignoring the exasperation he faked, and looked him over.

She leaned at the waist, spread her legs for him. This was the point. The swollen display that let him know he'd accomplished what he'd intended.

She watched the bells sway on their chains, just a few inches from the floor of the porcelain tub.

She picked up the dildo nestled in the powder-blue towel.

She put her left hand on the edge of the tub.

She grinned just a little and pushed back, just hard enough. The bells swung on their arc, and then crashed into the side of her tub.

Jingle, jingle.

She stayed where she was, bent over the tub, one hand on the side. She heard him rustle, stand, and she waited where she stood.

She heard him move. He stood behind her but didn't touch.

She held her breath.

She heard the belt buckle, the zipper. The whole mess hit the floor.

The hands rough on her hip.

He yanked her back and positioned himself against her slick folds, his cock hot and his patience betrayed, looking for the wet trap she'd set. He pulled on the chain, and she cried out in pain, desperate for something harsh.

He found what he was looking for, filling her to the hilt, and she dropped the dildo with a clang, bracing herself.

He fucked her roughly, knocking one leg out from under her. She buckled into the bathtub.

"You did that on purpose," he growled.

"Yes, Sir."

DEMICA

Tahira Iqbal

T ie me up." Those three little words had come out of the blue;
they had come breathlessly out of his mouth as he'd climaxed
inside of me. I must have misheard...surely my lovely fiancé of
just over six months wasn't into anything...kinky. Then, with
a quiet determination as he'd kissed me and ground his hips
against mine as my orgasm disappeared within, he'd said it
again, poised and with utter clarity. "Tie me up."

Now, one week later, I'm looking down at the card in
my hand that John had slid over the breakfast table the next
morning with a strong spark in his eyes that I hadn't seen in
a long while. I'd blamed my long working hours for the extin-
guishing of it. I guess I was wrong...the spark was from sharing
a personal secret.

I press the buzzer, the one marked with only a red star, and
wait.

"Yes?"

"I have an appointment for two thirty; my name is Eve
Nolan."

The door buzzes; I push it open.

My eyes adjust to the interior after the brightness of the afternoon. I'm faced with a staircase in a stark white lobby; there's nowhere to go but up. My sneakers stick to the polished wood floor until I hit the gleaming stone stairs. A door opens at the top.

"Welcome, Miss Nolan." says the smooth voice from the intercom, "Come in."

I shrug out of my jacket, the apprehension I'd been feeling during my journey to get here is raising my temperature significantly.

"Let me take that," she says with a smile.

I look around; the space is glamour. Nothing but glamour. The floor-to-ceiling sash windows are shaded with layers of pure white voile that move softly in the breeze. The floor is brilliantly polished tile, covered in places with white fur rugs.

There is a dazzling chandelier that hangs in long tendrils over a glass reception desk. Candles burn in clear votives along its length.

"Would you like something to drink?"

I stare at the beautiful woman as she stands with me, my jacket draped over her arm. She has an impossibly small waist, jet-black hair that falls in soft waves to her shoulders. Her lips are bright red, her skin milky pale. Her black clothes are elegant and clearly tailored as they fit like a second skin: pants and a shirt unbuttoned seductively so that I can see the lace of her matching bra.

"No, I'm fine, thank you."

She gestures for me to take a seat. I grab one of the magazines, flicking aimlessly through it, but I'm unable to think of anything but John as my heart patters in my chest.

"Just go, for me...please..." he'd begged.

"What if I don't like it...?" I'd been unable to hide my apprehension and fear as I'd wiped away my tears.

Since he'd said those words in bed, I'd retreated from him physically and emotionally as I dealt with it. Searching Google about his desires didn't help.

"Don't look at the Internet..." he'd chided softly, gently taking the laptop from me, "that's ninety-nine percent of what I don't want..."

I inhale deeply to bring myself back to the room. I love that man; have committed to marry him...I'll try...I can at least try.

I bury my head in the magazine for a few more minutes.

"Miss Nolan?"

My heart buzzes frantically. "Yes?"

"Demica is ready for you."

I'm escorted to a room. Expecting an office, I get a bedroom, the most stunning opulent space that I've ever seen, outfitted solely in white. From the shelter of the canopy over the king-size bed to the thick carpet that gives softly as I walk.

"Make yourself comfortable."

I nod dumbly, ambling to the middle of the room as she leaves. There's nowhere to sit except on the exquisitely dressed bed or the love seat by the shaded windows. I stand by the seat, grateful for the breeze from the open windows because my armpits are damp.

The door opens. My heart jumps into my throat again as a tall, slender woman practically *floats* in on sky-high heels, the seriously sharp toe peeking out from her black, billowing pants that rise up and skim her neat waist. Her ample breasts shift sensuously against the silk of her white shirt, the neck modest however, reaching up and ruffling just under her chin. Her black, poker-straight hair is tied at the base of her skull; the tail end of it swishing against her buttocks.

"Miss Nolan," she says, extending her hand, "I'm Demica, and I'm in charge of your induction today."

I swallow back the surprise as I take her perfectly manicured hand, the French tips gleaming. "This isn't what I imagined..."

"A dark dungeon with nothing but whips and chains?" She lifts her long, elegant hand to indicate the room, blood-red lips parting in a warm smile. "This is a much more conducive environment for training."

I gulp back my worry when Demica gestures for me to join her as she folds herself gracefully down onto the love seat.

"I'm a bit confused..." I mumble, clutching my bag on my lap, "I don't know anything about this...lifestyle..."

"Don't worry, you're in safe hands," Demica purrs softly, "Your fiancé is one of my most valued clients." Hearing it confirmed makes me sweat even more. "He's intimated very strongly what he would like to achieve from this."

"What about me...? Don't I get a say in all this?"

"Miss Nolan," Demica smiles, "you're the one with all the power, just remember that."

I hold my bag a little tighter.

"Now, the bathroom is through there; why don't you freshen up and change."

"Change?"

"I have picked some lingerie for you."

"Lingerie?"

"Miss Nolan, if you keep repeating what I say, we'll be here all day."

I rise hastily and clumsy fingers let go of my bag.

"Shit..."

I sink down to the fur, stuffing things back in.

"Miss Nolan...you can say no."

"I love him."

"Good. This is an act of trust, so we're halfway there."

I go to the bathroom, dump my bag on the counter, fighting tears. As I compose myself, I see in the reflection of the mirror a clothes rail filled with varying styles of lingerie all in green.

Green...my favorite color.

My emotions tumble within; he's shared secrets with a woman I didn't even know existed.

I pick through the rack, choked. There are elaborate creations from the biggest names in fashion and not one item has a price tag on it, but they are clearly brand new.

I look for a modest number, but there's nothing even close to my usual basic black...I pick a strapless bra but once I've put it on, it barely covers my nipples. I slide the matching high-cut panties on. I stare at the woman in the full-length mirror. Okay, so the workouts for the wedding are paying off...but...I can't. I'm about to haul them off and look for something else when there's a sharp knock at the door.

"Miss Nolan, it's time."

Shit.

I spray some deodorant on, grab the matching silk wrap that reaches midthigh and head out.

"There, that wasn't too difficult was it?"

I'm hot on my cheeks, feeling thoroughly exposed.

"That color really does suit you," she says, as she taps her finger against her lips, "but you're missing something..."

She reaches for a box that has been pushed under the bed out of sight and opens it.

I shake my head, "I don't wear heels that high..."

"You do now."

I take the black pumps...they are my size.

"How...?"

Demica just smiles. The knot in my stomach tightens.

John.

I slide them on, teetering a little as I adjust my posture.

"Take the gown off."

I don't hesitate. There is a sharpness to her voice that frightens me. And I want this over and done with as soon as possible.

"Hands to your hips."

I do as she asks, watching as she walks around me slowly, adjusting the bra straps, making my breasts lift. She alters the panties, her hands skimming my backside before trailing her fingers along the lace at the front.

"I don't understand why he didn't just talk to me," I whisper as I watch her, watching me, in the mirror opposite us. Her smile is dark, different from the welcome that I'd received earlier. Her eyes drop to my nipples, poking straight out through the lace and just visible at the top.

"He prefers action, as you will find out," she whispers into my ear, her decadent and heady perfume claiming my senses. "Come through please."

A door from within the room opens. I blush from my collarbones as a stark naked six-foot man walks in.

"This is Casper, and he is yours for the day."

"Excuse me?" I've already shimmied away from Demica and pulled the gown back, hastily tying the sash. I watch as Casper climbs onto the bed and lies flat out on his back.

Good god!

The man is bigger than John; his balls are neat and perfectly round and he's totally hairless, even his armpits.

"Look...I think I'd better..." I have visions of running up the street in this lingerie until I find a cab and probably breaking my ankle in the process.

Demica is unconcerned as she blindfolds Casper. He doesn't

protest; he just simply lifts his head toward her, accepting the white silk cover before sinking back down to get comfortable on the pillow.

"Come here."

I tremble where I stand.

"Come here, Miss Nolan, and take that gown off."

"I...I..."

"Miss Nolan, I won't ask again."

I slide out of it, feeling marginally better that the naked stranger can't see me... But oh, god...he's really naked! A naked, muscular, fine piece of work...

Demica takes his left hand, and using a restraint that looks like it belongs in a hospital, she locks him in.

My heart booms within.

"You can do the other one." She walks me round. "Take his hand." I look at her pleadingly. "Take his hand, Miss Nolan." I do, unable to hide the quiver in my fingers as I connect with his warm palm.

"Good, now take the restraint." On better inspection, I can see that it needs to be anchored to the wall where there is a metal plate with a semicircle welded onto it.

I look around the room I'm in. There are numerous plates studded around the room...some are even on the ceiling.

"Now, wrap it around his wrist...fasten this rope through the loop here and then to the wall..."

I do as she asks, but when Casper tests it, he's able to pull away.

"Knots are for next class then," Demica purrs.

Once we're done, I look at Casper: arms stretched wide, cock resting on his inner thigh.

We repeat the process for his feet, then Demica walks to a dresser and opens a drawer to lift out a black riding crop.

A cold chill drops from the nape of my neck to the base of my spine as Demica bends the crop daringly in both hands before handing it to me, "Miss Nolan, this play is all about sensation and taking it to such heights that the physical release you get with intercourse is heightened."

I swallow back a lump.

"Now, what do you think would be a natural move to make with this in your hand? Remembering that you are at the very start of play."

I put the crop on Casper's breastbone, winding it down in a lazy swirl.

The man ripples.

I whip the crop away, startled.

"Good, Miss Nolan, again."

Minutes rack up as I drag the crop in long, lazy loops across his body, letting it dip and tickle over his muscle definition.

"You've touched every part of him except his genitals."

I look at her, then Casper. He's halfway hard. I smile to myself as I put the crop on his lower abs. Casper moans in anticipation, his cock swelling magnificently. An incredible fire develops in my lower belly as I discover...*power.*

I adjust my stance, drawing my legs together as a strong sensation of wetness seeps through the delicate panties. Demica watches me like a hawk, a knowing smile on her lips.

I run the crop along his shaft, but it's difficult to maintain a connection as it bobs.

"Hold him, use your fingers instead."

The suggestion ruins the panties.

"You're not betraying John; he's approved of everything that we are doing today."

Those words are like a blow and must show physically, because Demica directs me to the bathroom again.

I splash cold water over my face, staring in the mirror. The bra and panties are on the wrong body...I don't suit this...I don't belong here.

But I love him.

I splash more cold water on my face, pat it dry and head back out.

Casper is now on his front, Demica tying the last bind before handing me the crop.

"Newcomers can get carried away with strikes in play, so be mindful. This..." she pats the crop against his buttcheek, "is soft, light...suggestive. This"—the crop cracks through the air connecting with Casper's buttock and making him moan while I jump out of my skin—"is business."

I stare at the flushed cheek, "What...what does John like...?"

"Miss Nolan, that is for you to find out." She hands me the crop. "Your turn."

I pat his butt lightly. Wet heat gathers on my inner thigh.

"Again," Demica says.

I pat him again, gradually increasing the tempo, but not pressure.

"Try a full stroke on the bedcover."

I do. The crop whistles through the air before it connects with the linens. Casper moans in anticipation making my nipples tingle.

I run the crop down his inner thigh, making Casper writhe. I whip the crop to the covers again. Something springs inside my chest when he groans my name unexpectedly. I'm expecting the cold rush of fear...but it's not there.

Demica's hands go to my shoulders.

"Do you want to know what it feels like?"

I look up at her, holding her challenging gaze for a few

seconds before I nod.

She unties Casper as I watch from the love seat. He's still hard.

"He didn't...you know..." I say to Demica quietly once he's left the room.

"You didn't say he could."

Oh.

"Come here, Miss Nolan." Demica draws me to one of the posts of the bed. "Up." She motions to my hands and my nervousness breaks out through every cell.

"I read something online about a safeword..." I gulp back my heartbeat.

"Excellent research Miss Nolan," Demica says with a smile. "In this play the safeword is 'ground.' You must use it if anything gets to be too much."

Quickly, she works the cuffs in place; they are soft, padded on the inside, similar to the ones we used on Casper.

I'm left hanging on my tiptoes in these awfully high heels. I keep my legs together hoping she can't see how wet I am.

"Uh-uh..." I get a tap from the crop on my knees before it works its way between my legs. I get the hint. I pull my legs apart.

"Why, Miss Nolan, I think you're enjoying your training."

I blush even more deeply than when I first saw Casper, as the riding crop snakes up my inner thigh. I suck my breath in as my body undulates. Something deep down inside springs into being.

The crop settles on the patch of fabric between my legs. Demica moves it back and forth achingly slowly. I let out a whimper and get a sharp crack from the crop against my thigh. "Oh!" My thigh explodes in pain from the blow. It certainly wasn't as hard as the one I'd delivered to the covers...but it's new to me and smarts like a bitch.

She reaches into my hair and unravels the band. My hair falls down beyond my shoulders.

I pull myself together.

And stand up straight.

The crop returns to the panties, going back and forth in a slow, methodical tease.

Her hand works the bra. It unclips, but she doesn't remove it; instead, she holds the cups and rubs them against my breasts. She might be lithe looking, but she's strong...her pressure flattens my nipples and a desperate ache breaks out across my lower belly.

She throws the bra to the love seat. The crop lightly taps my nipple in a succinct beat that makes me moan.

Crack!

The crop meets my thigh again. And this time the sting is multiplied and lingers deeply. The safeword vaults to the tip of my tongue.

She returns to the tapping, light and sure against my nipple.

Her fingers reach for the panties; she winds them into her fist, catching any slack. They're pulled hard against my clit and I bite my lip harder, desperate not to make a sound.

I hear something tear, the panties ripping away. I lower my head, staring down at my bared body. My thigh is burning, growing a deep shade of red. The crop works its way between my lips, immediately sliding in the wetness. The flat end of it rubs against my clit.

I start to shake.

The crop cracks my thigh and an explosive sob leaves my mouth.

Power.

It takes long minutes of silence to compose myself, and for the crop to come back to my clit.

I hold my nerve, close my eyes to allow the sensations to pummel me.

I start to come. It's basic, alive and begins from my core.

The crop starts to work harder. Faster. Faster.

"Hold yourself together Miss Nolan, you haven't been given permission yet."

I clamp my mouth shut, suck in my abs as the divine and very new pressure builds.

She taps the crop against my clit now.

"Climax, Miss Nolan, now."

The orgasm is barbaric, ripped from deep within a space I never knew existed, and is expelled with a scream of joy, frustration and salient understanding.

I wait, patient and pliant as she meanders beside me, searching my body. I know she can see my juices running to my knee.

"Well done, Miss Nolan."

She reaches up and unties me. My hands are tingling violently from the odd angle. I shake them roughly.

"Have a shower; the room is booked for another hour on John's account."

I slide into the gown, white-hot pain pulsing on my right thigh. It hurts. I'm not going to lie. She goes to lift the crop from the bed as I come strangely alive.

"Can I take that? The heels too?"

The tingles on my thigh vibrate upward, deep between my legs and into my core, broadening when I see Demica smile.

"Of course, Miss Nolan, I will put them on John's account."

"No," I say, standing as straight as I can, my nipples clearly visible through the silk wrap. "May I open one of my own, please?"

JACOB'S NOTE

Derek McDaniel

Julie came home from work that night to find what might have been the sweetest note Jacob had ever left for her. It was written on a sheet of vellum and sat, deliciously, upon their tightly made bed. The late-evening light was slanting through the windows, and when she flipped the light switch, nothing happened. She was left to regard the bedroom in ambient light.

There was a fresh comforter cover on the bed; the sheets and pillowcases, tomato red, had been freshly changed from the more typical, more prosaic ivory ones. Those were cotton; these were satin. There were three extra pillows, plainly new and very, very firm. These, too, were cased in red satin, but the fact that the three were stacked atop each other, midway between headboard and footboard, left no question in Julie's mind as to what they were for or what was intended to go atop them. The vellum note had been pinned to the pillows.

From each of the four corners of the heavy bed frame trailed loops of black nylon rope, open padlocks hooked around them.

She felt the ropes; they were quite secure.

Atop the white comforter between there were scattered rose petals. On the lower part of the rose-covered bed, south of the pillows and the note, there were two very large-looking dildos with a complicated array of straps, two pairs of padded restraints, a pair of silver-and-black nipple clamps joined by a bright silver chain, and a dog collar.

It was the dog collar, even more than the note, that made Julie's flesh feel tingly.

She breathed hard as she read the note again and again and again, hot waves of arousal pouring through her body.

There wasn't much to read, so each rendition was quick but nonetheless caused a whole new ripple of excitement to course through her. She read it so many times she lost track of time.

She couldn't resist the urge; she lifted her plain, businesslike wool skirt and slipped her hand in her panties.

Fuck, that felt good.

At that moment, Julie would have been happy if Jacob had shown up right then and fucked her brains out. No further preparation. No more ritual. No fucking around, just fucking. But that's not what the note said.

Julie really had to expend a lot of effort to get her hand out of her panties. She brought her fingers to her red-painted mouth and licked them, feeling filthy as she did. She unbuttoned her blouse, shrugged it off, put it in the immaculate, empty hamper. She unzipped her skirt, wriggled out of it. She kicked off her shoes; removed her bra, her stockings, her panties. She took off her makeup and got in the shower. On second thought, before her long dark curly hair hit the stream, she stepped out, dripping everywhere, and fetched a shower cap. The last thing she wanted was clammy, wet hair.

She got back in the shower, scrubbed her face, shaved. She did her legs and her pussy, her armpits. They were pretty much smooth, but it pays to be sure. She lathered and rinsed. The shower massager migrated down automatically, until she was slumped up against the clammy, cold tiles. Her eyes rolled back. She bit her lip. She had to stop herself.

She got out, toweled dry, shook out her hair. She looked at herself in the mirror and for a split second she was horrified. She *had* to wear makeup. She reached for the drawer, stopped. That's not what the note said.

Julie looked into the mirror again; she made a few faces. She pouted. She whimpered. She touched herself and moaned. She turned around, bent over, looked at her ass and her pussy over her shoulders—one shoulder after the other, trying to get herself from all angles. *All right, fine*, she decided. *No makeup.*

She went back into the bedroom.

By now, the bedroom was dim and it wasn't that easy to see what she was doing. But she knew the contours of the leather and metal like she knew the contours of her own sex.

The collar went first. Just the touch of it against her flesh was enough to feel electric. The sensation of it buckled around her neck was like a telephone call to her clit. She felt moist and slick, despite having soaped up and rinsed and toweled off just a moment ago. *Yeah*, she discovered with a quick, excited, vaguely guilty finger. *I'm already wet down there.*

She had always and would always think of the collar as a *dog collar*, because there was something fucking hot about being collared like a dog. She had purchased her very first collar at age nineteen from a pet store, blushing and squirming as the clerk rang it up, as if her shame-laced eyes could tell him she didn't really have a dog, and certainly not a hundred-and-ten-pound one. This collar, however, was *not* a dog collar—as evidenced by the added hasp, through which she fitted a padlock.

The lock on her collar gave a click as she closed it.

The gag came next, by simple necessity. It was shaped like a dildo, but broader and shorter than any dildo she'd ever be able to effectively fuck herself with. Its base fit into heavy strap that she secured around the back of her head.

The cock gag padlocked, too.

She had some trouble with the restraints, but it made her kind of hot to have to fight a little. She positioned herself face-down on the bed, softly cursing every aromatic rose petal her clumsy movements knocked on the floor. She liked them there, but this was more important. Briefly, after having to fight the first restraint—on her ankle—she changed her mind and rolled over on her back, positioning herself with the pillows beneath her ass. That was a hot position, but there was no fucking way she'd get her ankles restrained without herniating herself. She returned to her knees and finally got the restraints buckled, first around one ankle, then around the other. She fitted the padlocks through the hasps in the restraints, then hooked the black ropes through them. Each of the ropes trailed to a secure tie point on one of the bed frame's four corners.

With each sharp click of a padlock, she became more her husband's prisoner.

Jacob had thoughtfully given her almost no slack to work with. Once her ankles were shackled, her legs were staying spread until she was unfastened. She took a long, hot moment to position the pillows in just the right place—and then she spilled forward, over them, facedown, ass-up, very damned close to being helpless.

She had to attach her left wrist restraint to the bed first, of course, because Julie was right-handed. She buckled the right restraint before she did that—leaving the padlock hanging free.

Then she carefully secured the restraint around her left wrist and affixed it to the black rope tied to the bed frame.

Then she set about completing her bondage—fastening her right wrist to the bed. It wasn't easy. But what mostly gave her difficulty was her own impatience, and the tendency of her mind to wander over just what was going to happen to her as soon as she got that fucking padlock closed. She was intensely aroused. Her nipples felt so hard it almost hurt to let them touch the comforter. Her skin felt hot, but sweat was beading all over her naked body. The air of the bedroom felt chilly. She felt more moisture forming on her inner lips, and it wasn't sweat. Every grunt of exertion came out muffled by the cock gag in her mouth. Every helpless whimper, every squirm, every wriggle, made her hips pump and grind against the pillows. Each time she did that, she felt how tight her ankles were secured to the bed, how wide her legs were forcibly spread. Her ass worked with furious tension, arousal mounting. She felt trickles running down her thighs; Sweat, she felt sure. *I can't be* that *turned on, can I?*

She certainly felt very, *very* turned on, that was for sure.

The padlock clicked closed, securing the hasp of the wrist restraint around her right wrist, and to the black rope that locked her to the bed frame.

Julie moaned softly into the cock gag. Her hips began to grind as she struggled. *Yeah*, she decided. *I'm really that turned on.* She could feel it trickling down her thighs. She could feel her clit throbbing. She tried to hump herself forward and rub her clit against the pillow; she tried to bring her legs closer so she could maybe rub her thighs together. She couldn't; she was tied too tightly.

Then she heard him, below, heavy footed and menacing.

Had he been there the whole time? She would have heard him as she entered the house, surely. Was he out on the patio,

hiding? Was he outside the bedroom window, lurking in the
night, watching as she struggled? Did he come in while she was
showering?

Julie didn't care; she simply knew that Jacob was there. She
should have known he'd never leave her alone in the house to
tie herself up for him...hell, what if she'd had a heart attack or
something like that?

More importantly, there was no chance—no chance at all—
that he'd miss the sight of Julie locking herself to the bed. Face-
down, ass-up, spread, naked and sweaty and squirming, getting
more aroused with every process in the ritual of surrender.

The back of Julie's neck tingled to think that Jacob had been
there the whole time—but one thing she knew. He was there,
now. With her facedown, ass-up posture, she had to twist her
head around to see him—and still he was nothing more than a
shadow—big, bulky, menacing.

He didn't say a word.

Distantly, Julie heard the chirruping softness of clothes
hitting the floor, the clunk of wingtips kicked off carelessly.

Julie smelled his body as he circled the bed like a shark
approaching its prey. Her hips worked ceaselessly; she fought
against the bonds and heard Jacob's pleasured grumbles as he
watched her struggles augment her arousal. He felt her up and
found her wet. He slid his fingers into her, murmured approv-
ingly, took his fingers out. He drew his big hard hand back and
viciously spanked her. Julie squealed behind the bed.

She fought the alternating pleasure-and-pain assault of
his hand—the hand she'd been craving all day. She struggled
against the restraints she'd secured around her own limbs, the
ropes she'd locked them to.

He gave it to her hard again, again, no warm-up. He landed
his hand on her ass three times quickly—not a proper spanking,

but enough to get her attention. The sting and the thud pulsed through her naked body. Jacob put his fingers back in her cunt—three of them, now, almost too much for her...or just enough to stretch her. He started to thrust in rhythmically. Julie's eyes rolled back in her head as the big shadowy thing reached out, grabbed her hair, pulled.

He finger-fucked her right to the brink; when she was on the very edge, he withdrew his fingers.

Then she heard a buzz; without much warning, he touched a vibrator to her clit. She shrieked behind the gag. He almost pushed her over; he almost made her cum. She had been on the edge before—now she was tottering, ready to lose it.

He pulled away at the very last instant—so close, she almost thought he was going to get her off without meaning to.

Which would have been *fine* with her at that point—oh, she wanted it *bad*. But it was so much more delicious to be teased beyond the point where she could stand it.

Jacob switched off the vibe and set it on the bed nearby.

Julie felt Jacob's weight on the bed, bearing it down, making it jiggle. Every motion was excruciating; every touch made her tremble. His heat was all over her. She smelled his sweat. His naked body pressed up against her from behind. She felt his hand still in her hair, pulling. She felt his other hand coming down harder—much harder—on her ass, no warm-up, just a trio of strokes again—enough to get her attention...as if he didn't have it already!

He guided his cock to her slit; he teased her first with the stroke of his cockhead—then with another hard series of spanks. He ran his hands all over her hips, her thighs. He caressed her back. He tickled her. She jerked in bonds. He spanked her some more.

"Just what I like," growled Jacob fiercely, "a birthday girl who can follow instructions." It was the first thing he had said since he entered. Then he entered *her*, and the loud series of moans she uttered as he penetrated her told Jacob that his wife was having a very good birthday.

In fact, it was *such* a good birthday that when he brought the vibe to her clit, she exploded almost instantly; he felt her pussy clenching savagely around his cock as he fucked her. She came so hard the spasms of her muscles almost pushed him out of her. *Almost.*

He said, "Happy birthday, honey. And we're just getting started."

Julie moaned softly and tears trickled out of her eyes.

Jacob delivered long, rough strokes deep inside her. If she knew Jacob, the night really *was* just getting started.

Julie relaxed into her bound position, moaned into the dildo gag and let her husband take control. Jacob's note had been the best birthday card ever.

ANY LIGHTNESS BETWEEN BLACK AND WHITE

Dante Davidson

You seem confused."

I was standing in front of the wall of hankies, thinking, *Damn, there are a lot of screwy people out there*. When I say wall, I mean I was facing a fucking floor-to-ceiling wall of different-colored bandanas. Each bin was labeled with the code. Some of the labels made me hard—I'll say that right away. But others made me shake my head in wonder. Blue/teal = cock & ball torture (when worn on the left) or cock & ball torturee when worn on the right. I actually mouthed the word "toturee" as I'd never seen it written before. Mauve = "into navel worshippers" if worn on the left, or "has a navel fetish" if worn on the right.

Lavender meant "likes drag queens" on the left or "drag queen" if worn on the right. Would you really need a hanky for that? I wondered. Would a drag queen, all dolled up in finery, deign to wear a hanky?

I must have been standing by the wall for a while, because suddenly I felt a presence behind me.

"Need any assistance?" a man asked me, his voice an undeniably sexy rumble.

I turned my head, startled from my reverie. The stranger was tall and lean, dressed in dark jeans and a long-sleeved T-shirt. I wondered if there was a color for what he was offering—and if that imaginary hanky were worn on the left would it mean "provides assistance" and if worn on the right mean "needs assistance"? Clearly, I was out of my league.

The man smiled at me. He had a nice smile, dark curly hair, the type of gray eyes that have always made me think of stained glass—as if an inner light is shining through.

"Are you looking for something special?" he asked, and his voice caressed me once more. His fingers strolled through the different bins, lingering on the various "wants head/cocksucker" (light blue), "wears boxer shorts/likes boxer shorts" (paisley).

"How do people keep these things straight?" I asked.

"We don't get a lot of straight here," he said, grinning.

"No, really."

"There are a few main popular ones," he said, shrugging, "the rest are more for show."

"And the popular ones are...?"

He faced me again, and he said once more but in a more suggestive voice, "Are you looking for something special?"

When I first considered cruising the gay scene, I knew I would be at a deficit. Not only am I shy—ungodly shy—but I'm also color-blind. I don't mean that in the "we are the world" way—although I honestly don't care about a lover's nationality as long as there's chemistry. No, I mean, there are colors I can't see. Or colors I see wrong. So that if I were to walk into a bar and note a pale-blue hanky in a guy's back pocket, and think, *Oh, cocksucker*—I could be way off base. The blue might be pink, and I might accidentally pick up an "armpit freak," or a "cowboy's horse." Not that there's anything wrong with those desires—they just don't happen to be mine.

The hanky code—which could have helped me get around what my shyness prevented me from discovering—was truly the bane of my existence.

I lamented my problem to the stranger at the sex toy store in the Castro, and he asked matter-of-factly, "Why don't you simply buy a hanky, slip it into your back pocket and wait for the right man to find you?"

"I can't wait," I said, and I knew I sounded breathless. Then, worried, I asked, "Does that sound stupid?"

"No," he said, "it sounds honest. How long have you been in town?"

Was it that obvious? "Two days."

"What's your name?"

"Daniel."

"Daniel, I'm Lem." He took a step closer to me, and I could feel the heat coming off him. I was almost dizzy from our connection. Screw the colors, I wanted him to take me right there, kiss me, press me up against the wall of hankies and...

"What fetish were you looking for?" he asked.

I swallowed hard. I'm shy, like I said. And I have such a difficult time—have always had a difficult time—asking for what I want. But here it was, my chance. I wasn't going to let this go. "Bondage," I whispered.

He smiled and looked at me. "Gray." He didn't ask if I were bottom. He didn't have to. He took me from the wall of hankies and into the toys, grabbed up a few different devices, and then led me out the back door to his pickup truck.

"Don't you have to pay for those?"

"Not when you own the store," he said. We drove to his

house in the Marina, and when we got to the spot, he said, "You have a safeword?"

I shook my head.

"Let's go with *hanky*," he said, and he winked at me. He was obviously enjoying himself. I will admit that I was, too. My dick was rock hard in my 501s. But I was also nervous. I'd been craving this forever, and I didn't know what to do, how to move forward, what to say. My fantasies rarely featured much dialogue. I guess my fear was evident, because Lem put his hand on my back.

"Don't worry so much," he said, and he led me into his house and to his bedroom, and stripped me of my boots, jeans and shirt. He had me cuffed to his bed in a matter of minutes, my wrists anchored above me, my legs apart. My cock stood at attention, begging for release, but he ignored my erection.

"So you were looking for a hanky," he said.

"Yeah."

"Because you wanted someone to give you what you wanted."

I nodded.

"So what do you want?"

I rattled the chains. "This."

"What else?"

I'd rarely gotten past this image. My fantasies had almost always ended here, with me tied to a bed. The tying had been what was important. The being unable to go. Except I'd had to go far in order to get to this place. I'd had to leave my small, dull hometown in the Midwest, ride a bus for a miserable amount of hours, hole up in the cheapest hotel I could find, and then walk into a sex toy store in order to make my dreams come true.

Sure, there had been a few stolen kisses in my past. A drunken night behind a bar when a man I'd known forever made a move and I let him touch me. But I hadn't ever told anyone what I truly desired. I hadn't figured out how.

Lem said, "Use your imagination, boy. What next?"

I sighed and said, "Let me come."

"That's it? Bind you down and make you come? I don't think so…"

I closed my eyes. I tried to figure out what he'd want me to say. I saw the images in the magazines I'd been jerking off to for years. Lem came close to me. He kissed me and then bit my bottom lip hard, startling me with the pain. I opened my eyes and stared into his. "Daniel. What do you want me to do?"

I said, "Hurt me," and I felt my dick leak a little precome.

"Yes," he said, nodding. "That's what comes next."

He undid my ankles and wrists and easily flipped me on the mattress, cuffing my wrists back over my head. Then he retied my legs and stood at the side of the bed.

"We'll start with a paddle," he said. "Don't come on my sheets. I won't like that."

I sucked in my breath and waited. He started to spank me. As he did, he said, "Fuchsia's the hanky for those who like to be spanked. What color is fuchsia for you?"

"Gray," I murmured.

He spanked me harder and I worked to not buck my hips against the mattress. The friction of the position made me feel as if I might climax at any minute.

"Yellow is for people who like golden showers. What color is yellow for you?"

"Gray," I told him. I was having a harder time speaking now, and my cock was a living, beating muscle of desire. What would he say if I told him I couldn't hold back?

"Blue is oral sex," he said. "What's blue to you?"

I sighed, "Gray...I'm going to come."

"Not yet!" He dropped the paddle and climbed onto the mattress behind me. He undid my ankle restraints and pulled me up on my knees. I felt lube between my asscheeks, and I groaned as he slid one finger into my hole. "I'm going to fuck you," he said, adding another finger, stretching me open. "And then you can come."

I nodded at his words, thinking, *You'd better fuck me quick, then, because this is all too much for me.* He finger-fucked me a few more seconds, and then he was in motion, pressing the big head of his fat cock to my back door, giving me a second to grow accustomed to the sensation before slamming all the way home. I was crying at the way that he filled me up, the way he made me his. His cock rode me hard and fast. There wasn't a hanky color for what I was feeling—taken and used and fulfilled and needed. Or if there were, it would have been a rainbow.

"What color are your eyes?" I asked, suddenly needing to know. "Are they green or blue?"

"Gray," he said, and he reached his hand under my body and milked my dick for me until I was shooting, coming all over his fist and my belly and his sheets. I worried for a second, since he'd told me he wouldn't like that, but then I let the worry go. He was making me come after all. He shot his load a second later, filling me up with his spend, then pulling out and staring down at me. I didn't think he was going to let me go for a minute, but he did, undoing the cuffs and taking me with him into the shower.

"You wanted bondage," he said. "You came to a big city, looking for bondage, and you were lost, weren't you?"

I nodded. He was working the soap over me in the shower—his beautiful eyes smiling at me, his big hands roaming over my body.

"Poor baby," he said, kissing me under the spray, fisting my dick once more as the water rained down on us. "The hanky for bondage is gray," he said, and he started to laugh. "And when you looked at that wall, all you saw were fifty shades of..."

"Don't say it," I begged him, and I silenced his mouth with my own.

STAG BEETLE

Sacchi Green

She touched the little box in my pocket and smiled like an urchin sure of a treat from an indulgent uncle. "Is that my present from Japan?"

I gripped her wrist. "Is that a hand in my pocket, or are you just glad to see me?"

Kit, brow puckered, tried to puzzle out my mood. "Well, of course I'm glad to see you!" She tried to wriggle her fingers against my thigh. My grip tightened.

What am I doing with a girl too young to get a Mae West reference, even by way of Jessica Rabbit? "I'm glad to see you, too, Kitten." A warm, loving, beautiful girl. "I did bring you a present, but that isn't it. Careful now. Don't let the lid come off." I drew her hand slowly out of my pocket. The white box emerged, still intact, the thick rubber band now perilously close to one end.

"What..." Kit jerked an inquisitive finger abruptly back as the cardboard lid twitched from some inner movement. Her

expressive eyes widened as the significance of the tiny ventila-
tion holes sank in.

"Do you really want to see?" Kit had an involuntary horror
of creepy-crawly things. "My old students remembered that I'd
been interested in their collections when I taught there, and
thought it would make a fine present. I couldn't refuse. It was
an honor."

Kit had met me at the door wearing only a silk shirt, open
down the front; now she tucked her hands firmly under her
armpits as she hugged herself for comfort. "I don't know...
maybe..." She pulled herself together and let her arms drop to
her sides, body taut, scared-kitten face firming until it could
have been a smooth stone carving of Bastet. "If I don't see it, I'll
imagine something worse."

"That's my girl." Warm, loving, beautiful and smart. And
eager to please. I opened the box, my hand curved close just in
case. The stag beetle, two inches of black shell and another inch
of chitinous "antlers," peered over the edge. Kit inclined her
head just enough to get a good view, the trembling of her body
barely perceptible.

"They're quite beautiful, in their way. And harmless. I'll
keep him in a bigger box, a very safe box, and feed him fresh
fruit—bananas, mangos, sweet peaches." Was it accidental that
Kit's shirt slipped aside just enough to reveal the soft peach-
glow curve of her breast? A startling inner vision of the black
beetle moving across that sweet tender flesh sent tremors over
my body, too. "It's an ancient tradition for Japanese boys to
collect and breed stag beetles as pets. They're quiet and don't
take up much room." *Am I babbling? Don't overdo it, nitwit!*

"It was an honor, wasn't it?" Her hand came out slowly.
"Only boys keep them? It must be their way of honoring you as
Jess, instead of the Jessica they knew ten years ago."

"Yes." A tangle of emotions gripped me. Pride in her bravery fought with a need to push her limits, to see how much she could bear—and how much I could bear before nothing mattered but fucking her so hard she screamed like a wildcat.

"I want to hold him," Kit said. "Really." She held steady, the faintest of shivers rippling across the tender skin of her arm, while the beetle took a few steps along the back of her hand and wrist. She was pale and somewhat breathless, still frightened on a level logic couldn't reach. "I'm not sure I can hold still. Scary things...sometimes they feel so...so...I don't know. Maybe you could tie me up?"

"How did you guess the real present I brought?" I picked up my backpack and nudged her toward the bedroom. She lowered herself carefully until she sat on the bed, her back against the brass bars at its head, never looking away from the glossy black presence now innocently exploring her forearm—until she felt the wide silk obi wrap her tightly just below her breasts.

"Oh! How beautiful!" The delicate bamboo leaves embroidered on a pale gold background distracted her for just a moment, until I raised her arm to her chest. Her gasp shook the insect just a bit, and then he kept on, up over the mound of her breast. She was visibly shuddering now, barely keeping her hand from scrabbling at the beetle.

"There's a whole outfit in my suitcase to go with that, kimono and all," I said conversationally, while I tied her wrists securely to the bars with the ends of the long sash. She gave a sigh of relief when the bonds held however hard she strained at them.

"Thank you so much!" It didn't matter whether her gratitude was more for the gift, or the restraint. The relief vanished when the stag beetle crept along to her nipple and poised at its tip, feeling for a further foothold. "Jess..." Kit said tightly, then held her breath.

I reached out to reroute him, but she shook her head. "It's...
okay. Okay and...and awful at the same time." The beetle
turned back, revealing the nipple darkened from pink to rose,
and so temptingly erect that I could barely resist it.

A lovely flush lit her skin. No longer just struggling to please
me, she had crossed a line from fear to arousal, like pain giving
way to pleasure. Heat suffused my own body.

By the time the beetle descended between her breasts and
over her belly almost to her navel, she was whimpering, not so
much like a frightened kitten as a very hungry one. Her thighs
twitched, and her wrists strained at freedom, but she wouldn't
beg.

I was the first to give way. "No more!" I retrieved my new
pet, tucked him gently back into his box and set it on the nightstand. Then it was my hands that made her skin flush and thighs
dampen, and my not-so-harmless mouth that forced her nipples
to a rigid pleasure indistinguishable from pain, until her cunt
and clit needed all my attention and I drove her on from mewling
cries to howling release.

As we nestled close together afterward, catching our breaths,
Kit reached up with her now-freed hands to stroke my face.
"Isn't it a good thing," she said, with a mischievous twist to
her kiss-reddened lips, "that really, really scary things turn me
on?"

What am I doing with this warm, loving, beautiful, smart,
brave girl? Getting luckier than I'll ever deserve, that's what.

HANDS DOWN

Rachel Kramer Bussel

G retchen and I have a pretty conventional relationship, on the surface at least: we're in our late twenties, got married after a year of dating (three years ago); we plan on having kids; we both work high-pressure, high-power jobs in media, which often require late nights to meet deadlines. We look like young, fresh-scrubbed, all-American white yuppies—at least, that's what my brother in Santa Cruz, a tanned surfer with blond stubble and a laid-back attitude, tells me, when I see him at Christmastime. But what he doesn't know, and very few others do, is that beneath our sunny surface, we have a dark side. Maybe dark isn't the right word, exactly—*kinky* is. We like to play, and play hard, and after a long day, few things soothe me more than a nice cold beer and watching Gretchen writhe when I tie her to the bed, or a chair, or simply order her to stand against the wall while I beat her, and if she dares move, I shackle her wrists together and use a spreader bar to keep her in place. She loves playing just as much as I do, if not more.

Recently, though, I decided I wanted to do something a little bit new for us by taking our bondage play out into the world—the world of hip, downtown New York City. I would get to see a new side of my gorgeous, kinky wife, and see what happens when I unsettle her, shake things up, show her just how mischievous I—and she—can be. I didn't want us to be one of those couples who falls into a rut, even if it is a rut filled with spanking, bondage, dirty talk and rough sex. I wanted to bring our kind of sexy fun into an unknown arena, and our upcoming date night was the perfect opportunity.

We settle in at Joe's Pub, but as Gretchen's hand reaches for the menu, I tug it down under the table, as surreptitiously as I can. It's pretty dark where we're sitting; I'll need the candle to read the selections, not that I really care. My cock is getting harder by the second as I reach for her other hand and smoothly slip out her wraparound silver bracelet, the one I've tucked into my jacket pocket, winding it around her wrists. Ever since she bought it a few weeks ago, I've been intrigued with its erotic possibilities, and I've held it in my hands, twined it around my own wrists, marveled at how pliable the coils of silver are. It's almost as if the jewelry maker knew the potential "trouble" it could cause—if, by "trouble," I mean the most naughty of pleasures.

Before Gretchen can process what I've done, her hands are secured in her lap. She looks at me like she wants to laugh, or stick out her tongue, but I give her a calm smile and reach over to pinch her inner thigh. "I'll take care of you tonight; you just sit back and relax. Don't drink too much, though, because you're not getting up until the show's over." Of course I'm bluffing; if she's on the verge of having an accident, I'll let her get up, but she'll have to beg.

I make a deliberate show of reaching for the menus and

spreading Gretchen's open before her, since she's incapable of doing so herself. "You just tell me what you want," I say with a wink. I often advise her to tell me what she wants when we're in bed; she knows that ultimately I'm the one who will decide if she gets it or is made to wait. The look on her face is priceless; she can't decide whether to whine in protest or indulge in the arousal I'm sure is already starting. I tap my fingers against the table as I turn my menu over to look at the cocktails. Just the act of immobilizing my wife has me hard, like the air around us has changed, becoming charged with the tension my simple yet powerful act has provided. I'm tempted to twitch the tablecloth so the couple at the next table over can get a peek. Instead, I make my own selection and lean in close for Gretchen to tell me what she wants, but she just lets out a little moan.

"Like that, don't you?" I ask, even though I know the answer. "Just so we're clear, if you really need to escape, I'm sure a smart girl like you can figure out how to, but I'm also pretty sure a smart kinky slut like you wouldn't want to deprive herself of having me take care of you all night." The words make her breath catch, and I reach for her inner thigh and pinch it again to emphasize my warning. Feeling her smooth, soft skin with the pads of my fingers while the back of my hand brushes the bracelet makes me let out a deep breath, an image flashing in my mind of Gretchen bound with her hands behind her back, sucking me off under the table while I guide her with a hand in her hair. That's the thing about playing with her—one naughty action always leads to another, a dirty domino effect that I can't stop, not that I would want to.

Gretchen's eyes bug out even more when our waitress walks over, her waist-length black hair flying around her, revealing a glorious array of ink along her shoulders and back. She places water glasses on our table. "What can I get you?" she asks, pen poised at the ready.

"I'll have the antipasto platter and a mojito," I say, "and my wife will have the deviled eggs combination and a sparkling raspberry cosmopolitan." There are other items on the menu I know she'd have enjoyed, but these I can feed to her easily and inconspicuously, unlike the pasta or spinach salad, what she'd normally order. The waitress smiles at us and hurries off to place our orders, none the wiser to our little game, I don't think. I scoot closer to Gretchen and smile at her; the lighting is dim, but I can still tell she's blushing. "Having fun?" I whisper in her ear, keeping my mouth there so I can breathe against the sensitive area.

"I'm going to get you back for this," she says, though I'd bet money she doesn't mean it. Gretchen's a Type-A powerhouse at work, and sometimes it's hard for her to let go of work even when we're enjoying a night out. My job in our relationship is to force her hand—in this case, hands, literally, to relax. One thing I've learned about bondage over the years is that it doesn't work, in any form, if you tense up. For it to work its full magic, seducing both parties into the glorious give-and-take of possession and surrender, you can't fight it, which is one of the things I love best about restraining such an eager bottom; I'd never want to engage in bondage with an unwilling participant. Gretchen, though, was seemingly born for bondage. All it takes is a little bit of restraint, and it's like a switch is turned and she's ready for anything. The very act of keeping her still, locking her in place, prompts her mind to slip out of overthinking mode and her body to slip into full feeling mode. I'm not sure if she knows it, but there's a visible difference when she crosses over, submits not only to me, but to the adventure bondage promises. There's a little bit of her good-girl nature that resists every time, until the overwhelming need she has to be taken, controlled, and corralled wins out. If we were in a cartoon, this is when the lightbulb would go off over her head.

Sometimes I don't even tie her up at all, just order her to stay still, and then have fun with her. I'll tickle her, or spank her—sometimes I lick her pussy until she screams, as long as she stays in place; one small move on her part and I instantly stop, even if it pains me to do so. I can't do any of those things right now, so I take an ice cube from the glass of water in front of me and slide it along the side of her neck. "Don't want you to get overheated," I whisper. She giggles softly, and I'm thinking about how quickly this cube would melt if I placed it between her legs. Instead, I trail it along her cheek for a moment before casually slipping it into her lacy bra, the delicate lilac one I saw her slip on as she got dressed, when I had to grab her and bite each nipple through the lace before letting her return to getting ready. Thankfully her black top has enough coverage that I can get away with it without exposing either of us as inveterate perverts.

I pull back just as the lights go all the way down and the singer steps forward, pure glam with bold red lips that beckon to every corner of the room, blonde hair piled atop her head and what seems like a ball gown on, complete with a slit up the side, as she greets her audience. "I bet she'd know what to do with you," I whisper to Gretchen as I pick up another ice cube, this time slipping it under the table and into the palm of her hand. I press my palm against hers, feeling the dripping water melt against our skin.

If we were home, I'd surely take an ice cube and slide it along her pussy lips, tracing them until she squirmed and moaned, then press it inside her. I've done it before and it never fails to amuse me to watch her squirm, tightening around the cube, seeming to want to draw it deeper and expel it, processing the cold assault on her senses. And surely if, right now, her hands were free, the right one would be between my legs, teasing me, making me harder; she's as skilled at the subtle art of semipublic displays of affection as I am. I maneuver up her thankfully short skirt and manage to deposit the ice cube into her panties, just as I did in her bra earlier, and bring my fingers back to hers. She clasps one, digging her nails into my skin. The sharpness spikes its way through me, and I lean against her while the singer oozes seduction as she starts to sing—and strip. She's down to a gorgeous black camisole, black panties and garters attached to leopard-print stockings, by the time the first song ends, and I raise my hands above my head to clap, a sharp contrast to what Gretchen can do.

"Didn't you like that song, baby?" I ask softly, just as our waitress appears. Our water glasses are in the way, and I deliberately move each one as she sets the plates and cocktails before us. The waitress lingers for what feels like a moment too long, and the tension passes from Gretchen to me, but I know that for every actual bit of fear she feels, there's even more excitement. And it's not like we're doing anything illegal or even dangerous; she knows she can get away if she truly wants or needs to, and that I would help her do so if there were a fire drill or something. I would never do anything to harm her, and in fact, it's her willingness to do this, even when with a rustle of our tablecloth someone could easily catch on, that makes me truly excited.

I take Gretchen's drink and bring it to her lips, watching them part just enough for me to pour some chilled red liquid into her mouth. I picture the singer taking a turn feeding my beautiful wife and then it's no leap to picture my cock pressing between Gretchen's gorgeous lips, the singer stroking her hair. I set her glass down and take a sip of my own drink, before picking up my fork. "Hungry?" I ask, as my fingers drift into her lap, brushing against her makeshift bonds—I can't seem to stay away. The show only lasts an hour and a half, yet I'm the one finding the delicious agony almost interminable. The longer we sit here, the more I want Gretchen, in ways that are fully unfit for public consumption.

"I'm starving," she says with a smile, as the next set starts and the singer is back in a pale-pink sheath dress that clings to her perfectly. Gretchen and I have only had a threesome once, but talking about and checking out hot women sets her off. I pick up a deviled egg and bring it to her lips. As she takes a bite, out of the corner of my eye I see a woman at a nearby table looking at us, and I whisper as much to Gretchen. Whether or not this woman knows Gretchen's hands are secured in her lap, my feeding her is clearly risqué, even for this hip crowd.

"Do you want the whole thing?" I ask, as she savors the creamy confection. She opens wide and I push the rest of the egg between her lips, her tongue brushing my fingers in the process. I smile at the woman watching us, then give my full attention to the singer. She's beckoned a man onstage to help her change into an elaborate pair of heels, and he kisses the tops of her feet as he exits.

We keep watching as the blonde bombshell swoons and flirts her way through everyone from Marilyn Monroe to Britney Spears to Beyoncé. Gretchen doesn't know it, but I have a surprise for her when the singer asks for a female volunteer. Suddenly, I raise Gretchen's bound hands above her head, and immediately, the whoops and hollers from the neighboring tables cause her to look up at us, followed by a spotlight. "Oh my," giggles the singer. "You with your hands tied, get up here," she says. I pull Gretchen's hands down so I can undo the bracelet, but I quickly coil it around her arm and send her down to the stage.

I watch proudly as she gets a whooping round of applause,

and the singer admires the bracelet and even sticks out her wrists so Gretchen can show her how it works. Then they go behind a screen and the singer changes outfits while asking Gretchen questions, using the microphone so we can all listen to her responses. Hearing my wife confess to having had her hands bound beneath the table almost makes me come. When Gretchen returns to our table, I don't care who's looking anymore, and give her a full-on tongue kiss.

The show is winding down. We get the check, which also contains a note from our waitress saying, "HOT!!" I give a generous tip and lead Gretchen outside. "Let's take a cab," I say, even though we'd normally walk. I've already flagged one before she can protest. "Ladies first," I say, and once we're settled in, knowing I only have a few minutes, I reach for the bracelet and bring her hands behind her back. Soon her wrists are secured there, her body turned so she's facing the window, her back toward me.

"You were so damn hot in there tonight," I said. "I bet you had all the women jealous."

"I just hope nobody we know was there," she says, as if she really has some problem with it.

"So what if they were?" I ask.

I breathe hotly against her neck, and maneuver myself so she's close enough to feel how hard I am. We pull in, and I give the driver a thirteen-dollar tip on a seven-dollar fare. "I'll come around and let you out," I tell Gretchen, and then do so, lifting her up and keeping my arm around her, nudging the cab door closed with my hip. I walk behind her, my hand on her lower back, and guide her up to the elevator and into our apartment.

"You're wearing too many clothes," I tell her, easing down her skirt and panties. She wiggles out of them, and I can't resist reaching between her legs to make sure she's as wet as I've been imagining. No—she's wetter, and I ease two fingers in and out a few times until she moans and starts to buck back against me. "Later," I growl, and instead of going into the bedroom, I pull her onto the living room couch. "Now you get to see what that did to me," I say, as I slip off my pants and briefs to reveal my cock at full mast. "You're going to suck my cock the way I thought about you doing under the table tonight. Maybe next time I'll have you actually do it." I guide her to the ground, and pull her toward me so she's in the perfect sucking position. Watching her ease her tongue up my shaft, knowing she is achingly wet, hungry to have me fill her up and can't do anything about it, adds to my arousal. I let her get my cock nice and juicy, but when she goes to deep-throat me, I pull her upward by the hair. "Just the tip, baby," I order, and she dutifully runs that sweet tongue along the hard ridge of my cock. Her mouth is wet, too, the saliva dripping onto me, and the heat so intense I might come before I'm ready. When the sensation is almost too much, I pull her off of me and slap my cock against her cheek, making her moan.

The look she gives me is one of pure longing. "I know you love feeling me fuck your mouth, but I want to fuck that hot, tight pussy of yours." I'd been planning to finish in the bedroom, but I can't wait. I lean down and lift her up, settling her legs on either side of me, her wrists still secured behind her back. We've never fucked quite like this—usually she's bound to the bed, spread-eagled, but this is wickedly arousing too. I lift up her shirt and bite her nipples through the lace of the bra, while Gretchen raises her hips and slams herself down onto me. I bring my mouth to kiss her lips, her tongue racing to meet mine, and reach for her bound wrists behind her. I don't need to order her to come; I can feel the heat and trembling building inside her, and I crush her fingers in mine as the sensation builds before she collapses against me. "That's it, good girl," I tell her before I explode inside her. I ease the bracelet off her arms, letting it drop on the couch next to us, then pick her up and carry her into the bedroom. I pull her close, kissing her wrists, fully aware this has been one of our hottest date nights ever.

Later, before we drift off to sleep, I say, "You'll have to tell me the name of the store where you got that bracelet. I want to see what else they sell."

We both know we don't technically need any additional toys to embellish our bondage fun. All we really need is each other, but some extra help can never hurt. Plus, I know the perfect pair of nipple clamps she can wear while we shop. Now that we've ventured into "playing" in public, I certainly don't want to stop. The fun has only just begun.

SYLVIA'S TRANSGRESSION

Tamsin Flowers

I blame it on the weather. It had been raining intermittently all day and even when it stopped for an hour, the sky remained gray with no sign of the sun. Days like this are always bad for me; I'm at a loose end if I can't be working on my tan while he's out at work. Three days like this in a row and cabin fever's hitting hard.

So, as I say, it was down to the rubbish summer we were having. But maybe I was a little foolish to do it so close to his getting home. I didn't really allow any time for hiding the evidence, so I suppose, when push came to shove, I got my just deserts. And he did get back a little early....

I was still down in the kitchen when I heard his car pull into the drive. I ran up the stairs like a bat out of hell; if I'm not in position when he walks through the door, things can go wrong from the start. I made it into his bedroom and quickly stripped down to my bra and panties, shoving my jeans and tee under the bed. Then I lay down on my front on the bed with my arse hanging over the edge, just the way he likes to see me when he comes in from a hard day in the office.

I'd barely caught my breath when I heard his footfall on the stairs. I closed my eyes, willing myself to calm down. He couldn't know that I'd only just made it up here ahead of him. He liked me quiet and ready for him, waiting patiently in position with plenty of time to spare, not flustered and flushed. That would come later. I clamped my mouth tightly shut and breathed slowly in and out through my nose as I counted his steps along the landing.

The door handle clicked and then I sensed he was in the room, but I didn't dare look. No minor misdemeanors until I'd worked out what sort of day he'd had, what sort of mood he was in. God, I hoped it had been a good day so we could have some fun this evening. I hated it when he came in cross because of problems at work and took out his anger and frustration on me. The balance between pain and pleasure is a fine line, and when he's angry he takes me right to my very limits.

But today wasn't going to be like that. Please...

I waited, listening to him taking off his jacket and pulling off his tie. He hadn't said anything, but he often liked to keep me guessing. I pushed the front of my hips against the edge of the mattress to make my arse even rounder. I knew he found it irresistible. I could smell the day's sweat on him, mingling faintly with this morning's cologne. A hot shimmer of desire tightened deep within me.

I felt him sit on the edge of the bed and then his hand slipped inside my panties to caress my arse. His skin was warm against mine and his touch so soft... I pushed up against him but immediately regretted my action as his hand drew away. I knew I had to be completely limp; any sign of a response to him would result in punishment later and I still hadn't worked out what sort of mood he was in.

Suddenly he grabbed my right wrist and yanked my arm back hard. I gasped as a muscle tore in my shoulder, but that wasn't the worst of it. He sniffed my hand, my fingers; then he licked them. The air went out of my lungs as fear extended an icy grip around my chest.

"These fingers have been where they shouldn't have been, haven't they?"

I didn't dare answer, instead pressing my face into the duvet.

His hand was in my hair, pulling my head up. I winced.

"Haven't they?"

"Yes, Sir."

He let my head go and smelt my fingers again.

"It's not even you, is it? It's Merta I can smell on you, isn't it?"

"Yes, Sir." It was practically a sob.

If only I'd done it earlier in the day, so I would have had time to wash myself and get rid of the smell. What had possessed me and Merta to mess around just minutes before he was due home from work?

His weight lifted from the bed.

"I had a long day, Sylvia, and I'm tired." His voice sounded angry. It had that clipped, bitter tone that I'd learned to fear. "And now this, you thoughtless bitch. Move up the bed and take off your underwear."

I wriggled from where I was lying bent over the bottom of the bed up to the center, shimmying out of my panties and discarding my bra as I did. I knew what he was going to do. The cuffs jingled as he lifted them from each corner of the head-board and I held out my arms compliantly. I didn't want this; I didn't want to be hurt when he was angry with me. A moment later my ankles had been fitted with a spreader bar extended to its widest setting. I gasped a little as he strapped it on and instantly felt the weight of his hand across the back of my thigh. A sharp sting followed by a long, slow burn reminded me to keep my mouth shut.

I heard him leaving the room and wondered where he'd gone. I didn't have to wait long; two minutes later he came back in and there was a second set of steps with him.

"Come in, Merta," he said, as they both entered the room.

Merta was our maid. She was slim and pretty and spoke little English, and sometimes I couldn't resist touching her, especially if he'd left me feeling horny when he went out to work. She didn't seem to mind and never shied away from my exploring fingers.

I could sense them standing at the end of the bed.

"Show me, Merta, what she did to you. How she touched you."

A second later I felt a soft, feminine hand running up my thigh. I tried to stop my hips from moving in response to the dull ache that started up in my pussy. Her fingers stroked and caressed my buttcheeks as I'd done to hers and then silently slid down between them to push gently between my swollen labia. My breath was ragged and I clamped my jaws tightly together, even though I wanted to lift my head and groan out loud. The sensation of her cool fingers delving into my hot cunt was exquisite, and I knew that she would only have to slide them in and out a couple of times to bring me to the brink. But that would never be allowed.

"I see," he said. "Thank you, Merta. That will do. I will see to it that Miss Sylvia gets punished for her behavior."

I heard Merta leave the room and when she was gone I heard him locking the door. Panic bubbled up through my chest, and without realizing it I whimpered a little. His hand was in my hair in a second, gripping tightly, pulling my head back sharply.

"If you're going to be noisy, you know what will happen?"

"Yes, Sir," I whispered.

"Do you want to be gagged?"

"No, Sir."

"Are you sure?"

"I'm sure, Sir. I won't be noisy."

He slapped me sharply on the butt with a flat palm as if to test my resolve, but I was biting my lip and stayed quiet.

"Good girl."

I heard him pacing round the bed.

"Let's get this over with."

I lay wondering what sort of punishment he had in mind. Then his arm swooped under my waist and he pushed a bolster cushion in underneath me, drawing my legs up slightly and raising my arse a foot or so above the bed. I knew what that meant; with the spreader pulling my legs wide, my butthole and labia were fully exposed and vulnerable to whatever pain he devised for them. I shut my eyes and chewed on my tongue, determined not to cry.

He must have been aware of my distress because then I felt his hand gently stroking my arse and down the back of one thigh.

"Don't be frightened, sweet girl," he whispered in my ear. "You know I've got to do this for your own good. You know you'll feel much better when it's over."

"What will you use?" I managed to say, finishing with a slight sob.

"No, no, no. Nothing given away beforehand."

He moved silently in the darkening room and as the light faded, I felt as if I was losing myself, sliding into a deep pit from which I would never be able to claw free. All I could hear was his breathing, deeper and heavier than when he'd first come in. He was getting ready to punish me now, psyching himself up, deciding what he would use, how many times he would strike and how hard.

He opened the cupboard where he kept his toys and I heard him rifling through his collection: whips, crops, paddles, belts, a flogger.... He'd been collecting them for years and he'd tried them all out on me. I knew exactly how much pain each would cause and as I wondered which one he would pick, a dull, grinding ache of need made itself felt in my clit and my cunt and my arse. I breathed deeply; I was starting to sweat now with the anticipation. I wanted it to start, but I wanted to wait like this on the brink forever. I longed to hear the whoosh of air and feel the first the blow but I was scared, frightened of the pain, frightened of his anger and of his desire. I pressed my forehead into the bed as time seemed to stand still and all sensation was lost apart from the throb of longing that pulsed from my cunt through to my chest.

Then I heard it. The thin, high-pitched whine of his bamboo riding crop. Instantaneously, I felt it too; a shard of pain that seared through my left buttock and up to the base of my throat. I gasped, and then I wretched as the after-burn kicked in. I fought for breath, desperate to regain my equilibrium before the next inevitable blow. This was one of his favorites; a harsh bestower of pain, of bright red welts that stayed for longer than any others in a sharply delineated pattern.

"Look at you, you're so wet for it," he whispered near my ear and at that moment I became aware of hot juice that was dripping from my cunt and running down the inside of my thigh.

Swoosh!

And again. And again. A white-hot flood of pain. And soon I could no longer tell where the crop was falling on my bare arse—the whole area was swollen and burning. Until he lowered his aim slightly, and I felt the sting of the crop slicing across my labia. Exquisite, burning pain. A fire that cut through me like a laser and made me crush my face into the duvet to muffle my scream. He hit me there again and again, while I ground the soft fabric with my teeth, hardly able to breathe, my insides like a molten pool of lava. I was no longer conscious of the room or of him, or even of the individual blows. I was adrift in pain and breathlessness. Unable to articulate. No longer me. Just sensation.

Then suddenly the salvation of cold lotion. Two hands massaged the burning skin, fingers slid into my cunt, trans-porting me to the cusp between pain and pleasure. Seconds later, as I felt his hard cock power its way forward to my very depths, my world exploded and shattered with shock waves of pleasure. Now I let myself scream as he pulled himself back and plunged deep again. My legs were trembling, but he hooked an arm around me to keep me in position as he slammed into me again and again. With every wave of pleasure my muscles tightened around him, grasping his cock, pulling it in as he pulled it out and finally I felt the hot surge of his release as he groaned long and loud, still pumping hard for the duration of his orgasm.

He let go of me and I slumped forward on the cushion he'd put underneath me earlier. His cock, no longer hard, slipped out of me followed by a rush of hot semen running down my legs. I gasped for breath, once again feeling the pain he'd wrought as the pleasure subsided.

And suddenly I was swept, crying, into his arms as he care-fully took me across his lap, regardless of the sticky, dripping mess. I cried out in pain as my buttocks came to rest across the top of his thighs and he pulled me into his most tender embrace.

One hand pushed my sweaty fringe back from my forehead and then he kissed me, softly, tenderly and passionately on my lips.

Tears were still running down my cheeks, and he brushed them away with a gentle finger. I could smell my own juices still on his hand.

"Don't cry, sweet girl," he whispered, smiling at me with the softest eyes.

I sniffed loudly and burrowed my head against his shoulder.

"You feel better now, don't you?"

I nodded.

"Say it."

"Yes, Sir."

"And you know it was all for your own good, don't you?"

I kissed him timidly along his collarbone.

"Yes, Sir."

"So you won't put your naughty fingers into Merta's sweet pussy again, will you?"

"No, Sir. I promise I won't, Sir."

"If you do, you know what will happen, don't you?"

"Yes, Sir."

I sighed and he caressed my back. Then he gently pushed me down onto my front and applied more lotion to my pulsing, red cheeks. His hands slowly circled them with gentle, methodical movements. Despite the residual pain, the cool of the lotion and touch of his hands on my skin was blissful. Soon my belly tightened with desire once more and, as he heard my breathing come faster, he allowed a finger to slip into my cunt. He pushed it in deep until he found my G-spot and gently massaged it for a moment. It took little more than this to carry me off into that perfect dimension of overriding physical sensation. I came with a fierce cry and a spasm of arms and legs and back, and I heard him laugh at the pleasure he'd brought me.

This was my reward for taking my punishment and for promising not to transgress again.

But...if Sir really didn't want me to touch Merta, why did he insist that she carry out her duties in the shortest little skirt, without panties?

BODY TEMPERATURE

Thomas S. Roche

I'm pleased—and lucky—that Aisha doesn't see the cooler in the corner of the bedroom when I'm tying her up.

I don't want to blindfold her until it's done. I know she loves watching me do it. She gets off on the way I tie her. She stares with fascination and mounting arousal as I circle her body with rope, leaving certain parts exposed for my attention. I get her tits tied tight, but leave her nipples accessible.

I spread her legs and loop her lower thighs, securing them to the tie-downs at the base of the bed, but I leave her upper thighs—and her pussy, of course—nice and open.

Her temperature rises as she gets more turned on, and as I shroud her in rope. I'm not speaking metaphorically; our tiny bedroom was well over ninety degrees. We both were sweating our balls off. There, I'm speaking metaphorically...at least for one of us.

It had been more than a hundred all day, the tenth day in a nightmarish heat wave. Our tiny apartment doesn't have air-conditioning. Our window unit broke at the start of the season; our thrift-store swamp cooler broke after running for seven days straight. I won't go so far as to say we'd killed the goose that laid the golden egg, because a secondhand swamp cooler hardly craps out golden eggs. But if you believe in such things, you are welcome to say that our environmental careless-ness met with grim retribution from Mother Earth.

I get Aisha tied to the bed; she's red all over, dripping sweat. She looks both excited and angry; I can tell she's annoyed. The ropes make her hot; *everything* makes her hot.

And when she's hot, I'm hot. By the time this is over, she'll either kiss me or kill me. And in this heat, I'm basically fine with either.

The opportunity to stash the cooler came when a bitchy Aisha announced that she was going to take a shower, and I knew what she'd say when she got out. I was right.

"Did that cool you off?" I'd asked.

"No, damn it, I feel hotter than before."

It's what she always says, and her skin looked it. If I wasn't already familiar with how easily Aisha's pale skin got flushed, I would have worried she was heading toward heat stroke.

That's when I said, "I think I've got something that *will* help."

"Ugh," she said, waving me off. "I can't bear to be sweated on."

"I promise," I said, showing her the precut lengths of hemp rope. "You'll only sweat on yourself."

She looked at the bed, with its heavy frame. I had stripped the comforter off.

"Did you change the sheets?" she asked.

"Find out," I said, jerking my head toward the bed and dangling the ropes enticingly.

Aisha is a bondage freak. She's heavily into the idea of being bound when she doesn't want to be, while in all other matters— *all* other matters, believe me—being a willful, opinionated and highly vocal person. But when it comes to rope, a little adversity for me—that is, her own reluctance—really does it for her. She likes to be *convinced*.

Knowing this as intimately as I do, I found it indicative of just how fucking hot it was that Aisha had to think about it even for a second.

She finally said, "All right, but I'll safeword if you sweat on me."

"I would expect nothing less," I said. I spanked her ass. "Get on the bed."

We've got the windows open, fans blaring in the windows on high, but nothing helps. It's ten o'clock at night and just as hot outside as inside. Maybe at 3:00 a.m. Aisha or I will stand in front of one of the fans and make a soft sad sound of fleeting relief. But for now, every cubic inch of air within blowing distance is body temperature or hotter.

She's got pillows under her back, about six of them, which raise her frame to a forty-five-degree angle and give me the perfect canvas to work on. She's tightly tied, now, wrists to headboard, ankles to footboard, knees and thighs to the side rail and tits bound tight, distended painfully. Aisha has perfect breasts, the ideal size for her frame if you ask me, and frankly, she knows it. She loves it when they get attention, but nipple clamps and Tiger Balm only go so far—especially when every material or substance on her body makes her scowl.

And yet I've wrapped her in rope in a half-dozen places, the hemp rope like blankets. And I'll admit I'm getting off on making her suffer in the heat a little just to get her bondage fix. Her flesh is a vibrant pink, her face beginning to glisten. The scavenged yard thermometer in the living room says ninety-eight degrees—body temperature. But I'm certainly not telling her that. The merest mention of mathematical figures when temperatures over sixty are concerned is enough to make Aisha feel faint, and not in a good way. Is it ironic that her parents provided her with an Arabic name? No more than her pale Celtic skin or that dark Gallic mane that borders so beautifully on black. But if she ever does travel to the Middle East, I'm not going with her. I'll stay home and read her tweets about how fucking hot it is.

She's sweating, panting slightly; I can tell it's from a combination of temperature and arousal. The bondage is turning her on, all right, but she's fighting with the heat—the way she fights with it every minute of every day this time of year. She squirms a bit, fights against the bonds while I caress her; my fingers go up in her and I find out she's even more aroused than I thought she was.

She tries to lighten the mood. "Those damn fingers of yours better not be sweating on me!" She can barely get the quip out; it dribbles languidly from her lips, drunkenly. She's never been good at letting her tied-down status stifle her smart-assed complaints when I tie up her tits.

I respond with my thumb at the top of her slit, pressing in, feeling her cunt tighten up as I thumb her firm clit. I feel her telling inside, the gentle swell more intense as she tightens. Her hips move; I've tied them tight, but not *that* tight. She fucks herself onto my hand. I lean forward to kiss her.

"No sweating," she says, red-faced and glistening.

"I'm going to gag you now," I say dryly.

"Don't you dare!" she says. "Don't you know anything about dogs?"

"I don't follow," I say.

She speaks with difficulty, not because of the heat but because of the way my fingers are working inside her. "Dogs pant because they don't have sweat glands."

"But *you* have sweat glands," I say, dabbing my fingers in the pooling sweat pooled in the tiny hollow of her collarbone, just above the rope where I've tied her tits.

"No sweating on me!" she snaps, and I push the sweat-moistened fingers of my left hand into her mouth as I fuck my fingers harder into her, adjusting the angle to hit her at exactly the right spot. My thumb is tight and hard on her clit now; she's responding with little quivers and jerks of her bound, naked body. But she complains breathlessly, "Don't gag me."

"A blindfold, at least."

She likes blindfolds—she likes blindfolds a lot. She frowns.

She shakes her head. "I can't take another layer," she says, her voice choking up slightly as I finger her. "I almost cut off my hair today!"

I said, "Trust me?"

She scowls, rocking her hips.

"Okay. I'll try it."

"Close your eyes."

I have to say, "Keep 'em closed!" twice as I slide my fingers out of her, then kneel down beside the bed and open the cooler. If she recognizes the sound, she doesn't show it. I tell her again to keep her eyes closed as I get what I want and bring it back to bed.

She's really glistening now, covered. She smells fresh from the shower, but slightly musky from the heat. The scent of her pussy mingles with sweat. It's a wonder I can smell her over the unpleasant mingling of the tight, close, stale air of our apartment with the city stink from outside the window.

I set the plastic bowl on the nightstand and stand to the side—well out of sweating distance—as I blindfold her.

The blindfold was fresh and firm from twenty minutes in the freezer when I put it in the cooler as she showered. Now it's slightly less ready, but still cold as hell. The gel blindfold is one of those ones designed to take care of puffy eyelids, swollen tear ducts, bags under your eyes. It's the hungover debutante's best friend. This morning, I hid it in a Fudgsicle box so it would stay a surprise; when it's this damned hot, the last thing Aisha wants is chocolate.

The blindfold may have softened since it left the freezer, but in contrast to the air in the bedroom, it feels freezing—I can tell. By the time she opens her eyes in surprise, I've got the elastic around her. Her shoulders tip down, the small of her back up. Her ass leaves the sweat-soaked sheets. The ropes go taut. She wiggles.

I fetch an ice cube from the bowl on the nightstand.

I press the ice tight to the hot-pink side of her neck. I await that sound of scared surprise that I crave. She gives it to me— the gasp and the curse that says *You've blown my mind, baby.* It's followed by a pleasurable murmur, and she tips her head and presses her neck against the ice as I rub it all over her. If she had the faintest clue what was coming, she doesn't show it. It seemed like an obvious tactic to me; why I haven't thought about it before is utterly beyond me. But then, we both tend to lose brain function when the mercury hits these levels.

I stuff an ice cube in her mouth. Aisha sucks on it, crunches it up with her teeth. I've told her she'll fuck the enamel doing that, but tonight she gets special dispensation. She chews and sucks and moans softly while I fuck her harder with my fingers. I've reached over and retrieved another ice cube by now. This one makes its way across the exposed portions of her tightly bound tits. When it hits her nipples, Aisha curses, grits her teeth. I linger there. She shakes her head back and forth, coal-black hair dancing. Some plasters itself to her shoulders; I peel it away and brush it back. I ice each hard nipple in slow, tight circles and feel the pink buds harden. I zero in on one and plant my hand over her breast, ice cube in the hollow of my palm, until I have to grit my teeth, too. By then, she's pulling a Stevie Wonder, mouth dropped open and curses coming out. She can barely stand it. Her vocalizations go from curses and pleasured sounds to a high-pitched squeal of panic; then I palm the ice and shove it into her mouth.

There's not much left. She crunches. Impatient little slut.

I seize two cubes of ice. I kneel between Aisha's legs, acutely aware that I'm so overheated myself that I'm dripping sweat all over her. But this time she doesn't complain—at least, not about that. I run one ice cube delicately from her neck to her face, over her forehead, down the other side of her neck and across her collarbone to the tit I haven't abused yet. Its nipple's hard and sensitive already, stiffened in sympathy for the other. I circle it with the ice; when Aisha seems about to scream, I circle wider and let the melting cube orbit her breast at an altitude of maybe two inches. There's plenty to play with on Aisha's tits; I take my time drawing the ice along the edges of the rope, where her flesh distends. The whole time, I'm running the other cube up and down her thighs, first one and then the other. This necessitates an awkward cross-body placement of my arms that only makes me sweat harder. Droplets pour all over her. She either doesn't care or doesn't notice them in the waterfall of melted ice and her own sweat. The breeze from the fans is chilling us, now.

As I pop first one cube, then the other, into her mouth, I fetch two more and concentrate on her thighs and lower belly. I tease them closer to her sex, and she rocks her hips in time.

My cock is hard. It nudges her thigh, now and then, leaving a
tiny trail of precum. I lean forward so I can caress her tits and
her face and her neck again with both half-melted cubes. I don't
quite touch my thighs to hers, lest I sweat on her. But the head
of my cock grazes her sex.

"Fuck me," she gulps.

"I'll sweat," I quip.

"Shut up and fuck me," she says.

"Not just yet," I tell her, nudging the tip of my cock just
barely into her; she gasps as it penetrates her, but then I pull
it back at the last second. I bring my hands down to her pussy
and slide the ice up the narrow space between her lips and her
thighs. She moans.

These two cubes are mostly melted, now, and it's damn hard
to hold them. They could slip from my fingers at any time. So
I put them somewhere they won't get lost. I stuff them both
inside her.

That brings a howl from Aisha. Her shoulders go down hard
against the pillows, the small of her back forming a parabola
as she strains against the ropes, surges and trembles against the
sensation. I enter her quickly, feeling the tightness that comes
from her natural, slippery lubricant being watered down as her
pussy melts the ice. There's still enough of it remaining that
when I thrust quickly into her, my cockhead meets the remnants
of first one, then the other mostly melted cube on its journey
to the sensitive place near her cervix. I know from the way her
mouth drops open wide that the pressure on that spot is making
her eyes roll back behind the gel blindfold. She's moaning.

Caught off guard by the cold, her sex has tightened; it
feels uncharacteristically snug and unwelcoming against my
thrusts—not to mention painfully chilly. Aisha seems to like
that. But it's my thumb on her clit that finally pushes her over the

edge—no refrigeration necessary. I even warm it in my mouth before I press it up against her to stroke her clit in concert with my thrusts.

By the time I come, I'm sweating all over her; great drops of my perspiration pour from my body and soak the ropes alongside Aisha's own sweat. Her skin is slick from top to bottom, with sweat and water.

She makes pleased sounds as I come inside her. I think I know better than to slump atop her—but when I try to pull back, she fights the bonds to pull her thighs together. She tries to trap me.

I get the picture; I lunge forward, my body against hers. She's breathing hard and not from the heat. Her teeth are almost chattering.

"You're shivering," I tell her.

"So warm me up," she says.

Her mouth surges up to kiss me, and for a long time I sweat all over her. She doesn't shiver for long.

CAMWHORE

Auburn Sanders

She starts out wearing low-front, see-through mesh panties because she likes the way the angle of the panties seems to slim her wide hips and the way the transparent mesh accentuates the smoothness of her pussy. She wears a heavy bondage belt around her waist even though it makes her sweat, because there's no convenient way she can attach her leather restraints above her head without taking about a year and a half's worth of yoga. And she wears a push-up bra a cup size too small because she loves the way the push-up bra elevates her tits, making them spill out over the tops of the cups and providing ideal purchase for the clothespins.

She curses as she puts another one on—her twelfth, and that's just on her left tit. Three run down the left side, low, sticking almost straight over her armpit. Three stick at an angle over her right breast. Three more go along the underside of her ample tit, angled up over her rib cage, and she's just applied the third of the three that stick up from the top, pointing at her chin.

The D-rings of her leather wrist restraints rattle as she moves her hands. It's awkward with them on, but she loves the way they look. More importantly, she loves the way they feel.

The D-rings snag against one of the clothespins. She yelps and jerks. She sees her laptop sway back and forth. She's half afraid she's going to kick it over, but it stabilizes.

She takes three more clothespins from the box by her bed. She puts them on between wriggles and moans and soft, shallow sobs. One to the inside, one to the outside, and then—both tits heaving from her great ragged breaths of pain—she whimpers and moans as she puts on the last one, right in the center, sticking out straight and screamingly painful.

"Fuck, oh fuck, oh fuck fuck fuck," she says, shaking her head to clear the pain. It undulates through her body, making her arch her back and prop herself up on her left hand. It makes her grind back and forth, rubbing her panty-clad ass against her dirty sheets in a vain attempt to sooth herself, to distract herself from the agonizing pain in her tits.

What distracts her far more than the sensuous feel of her ass against the sheets is the tight embrace of the heavy padded restraints on her ankles. They're secured by spring clips and chains to the metal frame of her full-size bed. They rattle a little when she squirms, which is why she wishes she could play music. But she can't, or she wouldn't be able to hear the sound from her laptop, which is propped on a pillow between her forced-apart knees.

She looks at the screen. She moans. She says, "Oh, fuck, that hurts. That fucking hurts."

She just keeps saying it and looking at the screen as the pain rumbles through her body. She breathes deep and hard and pulls at the tightness of her ankle restraints. She runs her hand up her neck and feels the thick leather collar with its heavy silver D-ring and the silver chain leash tossed over her shoulder. She tugs at it.

So what if it hurts, slut, someone says in her mind. *You like it. You know you fucking like it.*

She sees a hand reaching for a cock. She smiles and slaps her face. A hand grips a cock firmly. It doesn't move. She slaps her face again, harder this time, and makes a pathetic whining noise. She pulls at her leash, runs her hand over her collar, slaps her face even harder, pulls at her collar and the leash.

The hand moves faster. She smiles.

Fifteen clothespins radiate out from her upthrust left breast, like a porcupine's quills, only she's not sure if she's the porcupine or the victim. The clothespins bite into her flesh; she can barely take it. A wave of sensation crashes through her body and she almost loses it. She panics, gasps, sobs, reaches for the one in her nipple to pluck it away; it's more than she can stand. Her fingers stop before she removes it. Her fingertips almost touch the clothespin—almost, but not quite. She leaves it there, shivering for an instant as she waits to see if she can handle it. Then she breathes out long and slow and leaves the clothespin where it is.

Her fingers tremble as she reaches for more.

She takes three more clothespins from the box beside her bed; one goes on her right breast, down on the tender part where the push-up bra lifts it up tight. She pinches to get purchase, moans softly as she centers the pin. She leaves it and adds another alongside it. She's less symmetrical now, not caring where they go, exactly—just that they get placed. She picks up speed. She has to cross-reach over her upper belly to pinch her right tit properly; she dislodges one of the clothespins and shrieks. She curses herself for the noise she made; she's got motherfucking roommates. *Quiet, bitch. Don't make a sound,* someone says in her mind. She shoves her hand down into the black mesh panties and rubs herself. She thrills to the smooth feeling. *Nice and smooth, bitch...you shave your cunt. What are you, a hooker? A porn star?*

In fact, she isn't a hooker, and she's probably not a porn star. But when she looks down to the screen of her laptop, she sees a hand moving faster on a cock, and she likes that. She likes that a lot.

In her mind, someone sneers, *You're making him jack it, slut. A stranger's jacking off to you hurting yourself, and you like it. What a sick perverted cunt you are. You should just charge him a flat rate and have someone pack you up and ship you to this asshole to live as his sex slave. He'd probably hurt you all the time, then; would you like that? You wouldn't have to hurt yourself, then...would that be more or less perverted?*

She grunts as she puts on a fourth, fifth, sixth clothespin. Her breasts heave harder and deeper as she breathes deeper and with greater urgency. She has to remind herself not to hyperventilate. Soon only her right nipple is free.

On the screen of her laptop, the hand has stopped moving on the cock; now it's tugging at a swollen pair of balls hanging out of a set of boxers. *He's trying to make himself last*, she thinks, and someone says loud in her brain. *He's trying to get his money's worth. He paid for thirty. He doesn't want to cum yet. Do you want him to cum so you don't have to do this anymore? Or do you want him to watch?*

She moves fast to put the three clothespins on her nipples; she's starting to fly from the pain, feeling suddenly hungry for it.

She looks at her laptop. The hand is pulling at balls. She grabs her collar, pulls, slaps her face three times in quick, rapid strokes.

The hand goes back to the cock. She watches as he pumps

furiously—then stops. His fingers go back to his balls. She feels a rush of excitement.

She fumbles the ball gag out of the box by her bed. Did she wash it after the last time? She doesn't care. It tastes rubbery, dusty. It's awkward trying to move around with the D-rings of her wrist restraints dangling against the clothespins. She can barely move. If she wasn't propped up on pillows, she wouldn't even be able to see her laptop behind the irregular curtain of clothespins. Then she wouldn't know that when she shoves the ball gag in her mouth, the hand starts pumping cock hard and fast again.

It doesn't last long; maybe three strokes, then he's furiously back to his balls, pulling them down. *Why do some guys do that?* she wonders. *Does it really make them last?*

You want him to last, slut. You want him here with you when you cum. What good is a nice hard cum if you don't get paid for it?

Awkwardly, she buckles the black leather strap of the ball gag behind her head. She dislodges two clothespins as she does it; pain surges through the distended flesh where they left deep impressions. She howls in pain. She likes the way the ball gag makes it sound; screw the roommates.

She squirms back and forth, rattling the chains that lead from her ankles to the cheap metal bed rail. She brings her left hand down alongside her bondage belt and awkwardly works the spring clip until her wrist restraint is tightly secured to the belt. She does the same with her right wrist—but not before she does something else.

She's got the vibrator ready, next to the bed. All she's got to do is tug on the cord and it comes up easy. She spreads her thighs as wide as she can. The vibrator is one of those long models—the kind with a big broad head and a long handle.

She shoves it down into her panties and turns it on.

She presses her thighs together to trap it. She moans into the ball gag; her back arches; she throws her head back and shakes from side to side. The whole bed rumbles in response. When she sits up again, her laptop is tipping awkwardly back and forth, almost falling off the pillow. But the hand is pumping furiously, and she gives it a big wet look from her big wet eyes and starts fucking her hips against the vibrator.

She stops moving her hips, pushes her thighs more tightly together and lets go of the handle. She twists her hand around and works the spring clip to the D-ring of the belt. She reaches up again, flailing with her fingers, and grabs the handle of the vibrator again. She pulls at the belt with both her wrists— the left so it looks like she's struggling; the right so she can open her legs and push the vibe down deep and fuck herself against it.

Onscreen, the hand is moving faster, leaving the cock more and more. Every few strokes the hand stops and reaches down to pull at the swollen balls. She feels a thrill each time it departs, each time it returns. *He's jacking himself, slut. He's going to cum. He's gotta stop jacking himself, slut...he doesn't want to cum yet. Look at him pulling his balls. Look what you make him do. You make it so he can't keep himself from cumming. He's gonna blow his load and it's all your fault, bitch. What a horny, slutty cunt you are. What an irresistible little bondage slut. I bet you want to see it, don't you? See his big hot load shooting everywhere?*

She doesn't; she doesn't care. She doesn't give a damn if she sees it or not. What she likes is his hand moving fast and desperate trying to make his cock shoot, and then stopping and pulling at his balls trying to make himself last. *But he can't. He can't last, slut. He's too fucking hot for you, little bondage slut.*

You're his camwhore. You're making him jack himself off. He wants to stop but he can't. It's all your fault.

She's close. She shrieks and pushes her hips up into the air, lifting her butt off the sweat-sodden bed and pressing her thighs together. She throws her head back. Her hair is everywhere. Clothespins go popping as she gag-screams and writhes. Pain floods the deep imprints left by the clothespins.

She goes rigid. She cums hard. Her pussy contracts; her body goes hot-cold-hot-cold with blasts of pleasure. She screams into the gag. All that comes out is a muffled sound. Thank god; her motherfucking roommates are probably already wondering what the fuck all that rattling is.

Her ass pumps hard for a minute; it lowers to the wet bed. She opens her thighs and pulls the vibrator out of her panties. She flips the switch, tosses the vibe to the side. It hits the floor and the switch goes on again. It rattles there, buzzing on hardwood.

On her laptop, the cam window's empty except for the little thumbnail that shows her with her legs spread and her tits like porcupines. The guy is gone. Did he cum? There's no way to tell. She didn't really want to see it, but she wishes she knew one way or the other.

With some significant effort, she unfastens the spring clip attaching her right wrist restraint to her bondage belt. She reaches over and frees her left wrist. She undoes both buckles impatiently; her wrists are sweating.

Her stomach is sweating, too. She's sweating all over. She unbuckles her bondage belt and tosses it irritably on the floor. She takes off her gag and leaves it on the sweat-soaked pillow beside her.

She looks down at her tits, which are heaving from her deep, desperate breaths. They always hurt more coming off than going on. It's one of the reasons she likes them.

But she's never worn this many before; she's never had a client who asked her to wear so many. And it's probably been almost twenty minutes since she put on the first one. She never leaves them on that long.

In her head, she hears her nasty voice.

That means it's really going to hurt, slut, taking those fucking things off. The longer you wait, the more it hurts. What is that, like thirty of them? Nah, you lost a few...there's still like twenty-five left. Damn, that's gonna hurt. You're probably gonna cry. You'll definitely scream. You'll probably like it. You just wish you had some guy to watch you, don't you?

She's humming with terrified anticipation as she takes deep breaths, porcupine tits heaving. She reaches for the first clothespin.

Her laptop chimes. She sees a chat flag.

She sits up awkwardly, feeling the wetness under her butt and the pull of her flesh against the clothespins. She leans forward.

She sees her own image distorted through the fish-eye lens of the cam. Sweat coats her face, as it does her whole body. Her mascara's everywhere; black drops of it dot the wooden clothespins. Her lipstick's ruined. Why does she even wear makeup for these things?

She double-clicks the chat flag. It's a new user—one she's never heard from before.

I see from your profile you like clothespins, the message says.

She takes a series of deep, quick breaths; she looks down at her tits and trembles in a softly familiar blend of terror and pleasure.

She shifts her ankles, feeling the embrace of the restraints, hearing the rattle of the chains.

She wipes her hands on her sheets. She types:

I sure do. In fact, I'm wearing about twenty-five of them on my tits right now. Wanna see me take 'em off?

She makes a smiley face. She *never* makes a smiley face.

She breathes deep and hard as a long moment passes.

Then she hears another chime, sees the credits rack up in her profile. Twenty more minutes, prepaid. A half-hard dick appears on the screen, a hand furiously pulling at it.

So you've been a nasty little fuckwhore, says the voice in her head. *Let's see you hurt yourself.*

She reaches for her ball gag and stuffs her mouth full. She buckles it tight, tucks her left hand under her tit and lifts it up.

She plucks away clothespins. The hand moves faster. She bites down on the gag and lifts her butt off the sweat-soaked sheets.

TWISTED REALITIES

Kiki DeLovely

M y first four, semilucid nights at Misericordia Hospital were spent in a haze, and for that reason I was unsure as to whether or not I had imagined him. So picturesque, dark curls offsetting his hazel eyes, an exquisite blend of feminine and masculine, he looked like he had walked off the *GQ* pages of my dreams and materialized by my bedside to check my vitals. I could only recall brief flashes of him coming and going. I heard his voice, reading something about a woman too disturbingly beautiful for this world, how she ascends into the heavens, and then his words faded away in the distance. I saw him taking a syringe to my drip line and then everything went blank. I even thought I could recall his scent, trailing off into the night. My body—a much more reliable source than my mind at this point—distinctly remembered feeling how he positioned himself on the edge of my bed one night, the heat of his thigh pressing up against mine. Then gone.

Surely it had to be the drugs.

My memory could not quite piece together the facts

surrounding my accident either. The rain was coming down hard and so I didn't see the big cat until the very last second. Her gold-brown eyes staring at me through the droplets on the windshield, confused as to why I would disturb her moment of peace as she stood, unflinchingly stoic in the middle of the road. I flinched, swerved, felt the car gliding along the slick pathway and then everything spinning in slow motion. But that's all I could recollect. The doctors informed me that the car rolled several times. The air bags saved me from death, but my head hit the side window hard enough to knock me out for a couple of days. Even when I regained consciousness, I was still in and out with little, if any, warning. Between the skull-numbing pain and the drugs they fed me to keep the worst at bay, I couldn't trust myself to distinguish reality from dream. Then there was the layer of surreality surrounding my gaze-divertingly hot nurse. Gabriel.

On the fifth day of this bedridden state, I resolved to approach the evening with a clear head. Or at least as clear as my concussed brain would allow. I refused the pain meds they tried to push on me so that I could be cognizant of Gabriel's late-night visitation. I had to know that he was real. Perhaps he wasn't? But that's about as far as I could let my imagination wander. Had I been in my right mind, I wouldn't have even taken it that far.

I awoke to his light eyes peering intently into mine. *Mierda. I must've drifted off.*

"How's the pain, *cielita?*" Glancing down at my chart, he continued, "I see you've been refusing the Dilaudid."

Somewhat taken aback at the immediate intimacy of his stare penetrating me upon waking—the feeling of him inside me even before my first thought could form—it took me a second to put words together. "I'm still trying to find my way out of the haze.

At moments, I felt like I was losing my hold on reality. I just want to think straight. Without the drugs, the pain is certainly keeping me bound to reality. I hope."

Gabriel began nodding at my mention of grogginess, letting me know that he understood. He didn't see anything unusual about my choice to take on the pain for clairity's sake, unlike the other nurses. Rather, he respected it. I sensed that he thought it wise and actually quite reasonable.

"You've been able to sleep despite the intensity of the headaches, so that's a good sign."

"I've actually grown somewhat accustomed to the maladies in my head..." I spotted the slightest shift in his facial expression and I crumbled. "Oh, god, I used that word incorrectly, didn't I? How embarrassing." I launched into a babble about how it's all still quite fuzzy and I know it's nothing in comparison to a severe head injury but I've been having these damn leg cramps at night that wake me just when I seem to drift off, and I heard my voice and recognized how ridiculous I sounded. Why the hell was I telling him this? My mouth kept flapping and I beseeched my brain to please stop.

Rescuing me from the red-hot flushing across my face and my mouth that wouldn't seem to quit, no matter how much I willed it, Gabriel broke in, "Why don't you let me see what I can do to keep your calves from tensing up?"

Not waiting for my consent, he reached for my legs. He slowly peeled back the stark white hospital bedding until just the edge of my thigh was exposed. He gripped just past my knee and began massaging me there. Gabriel took his time working out the soreness, digging into my atrophied muscles firmly, hurling me into delectation. As he brought needed relief to my legs, it felt as though he was sending every last drop of blood in my veins directly to my clit. I began to throb. Hard. So hard I feared that he might be able to hear it. I couldn't help but stare at the thick vein in his neck that seemed to be pulsating in time with my licentious heartbeat.

"I have to admit, I'm delighted to have you so lucid tonight. It feels a little…selfish." Gabriel stopped himself, but I couldn't muster the courage to ask him why. After a while he spoke again, telling me that this was his last night at Misericordia. He was involved with a program that transferred him all over the world and he'd be heading to Aracataca, a small river town near Soledad in Colombia's Caribbean region, the very next day.

"I know you haven't exactly been coherent for most of our conversations, but I wanted to thank you because for the first time since I got here, I haven't felt alone. There's something… comforting about you…." His voice trailed off so I could hardly make out the last bit, "…and deeply provocative."

As he'd just barely uttered those last three words, the air sparked, igniting a palpable intensity between us, and I felt all my inhibitions fall away. They hit the floor, shattered into a hundred indecipherable fragments and dissipated into the atmosphere, as if they had never existed. Usually, I bury my passions in exchange for practicality. I resist ever getting swept up in a moment, never one to indulge in lustful craving. And yet here I was, sitting in a fucking hospital bed, ready to tear off this god-awful nightgown, rip out my IV with my teeth, and devour this most sumptuous of men.

Fuck. I have to get a hold of myself.

I allowed myself a sideways glance at him and immediately felt the pull of a skydiver's traction, the pressure of oxygen pushing up against its tank, the skin stretched taught across a firefighter's healing burns. I perceived every single bit of tension in this hospital straining against the space between us.

"I want to subdue the rest of your pain." And with that,

again needing no permission, his hand crept up over my knee. Trailing along my inner thigh with just his fingertips, Gabriel blanketed my skin with goose bumps.

My heart surging and breath short, I couldn't look at him. I looked down at the sea of white that covered my body, distancing me from myself. Although utterly responsive, I was outside of it all, as if I was looking down on something that was happening to me, instead of being an active participant. Or at least a willing recipient. I watched intently at how the sheet rose and fell, undulating like waves in the wake of his hand as it gradually made its ascent toward my cunt.

I wanted to scream, but not out of pleasure. I was dying to drive a crack in this pristine surface, to scream out in protest at the top of my lungs, to struggle and fight him off, to push away this satisfaction that I needed so desperately. This desire that I had to have. Still I wanted to scream. I opened my mouth but instead only a moan escaped as I felt his fingers glide across my rain-slicked path, causing time to slow, the room to spin. I gasped at the shock of his fingers, the arousal that grabbed hold, the pain that shot behind my eyes.

"I'm going to need you to be a good girl for me and be very, very quiet. No one can know about this. We can't risk anyone hearing...."

This awakened an altogether new, more depraved level of excitement in me and without warning, someone—far more brash than me, much bolder and inexplicably crude—someone else's words were rolling off my tongue. "One scream from me and you could lose your license. You've got my DNA smeared all over your fingers and I'm a defenseless, drugged-up, concussed crash victim. It wouldn't look good, would it?" I witnessed a lustful abyss pooling in his eyes. "So you're gonna want to do exactly as I say."

Where was this coming from? I knew that I'd hit my head pretty damn hard in the accident, but what the hell had come over me?

I had started down this path, seemingly, of my own volition; guided by some inner drive, some deep-seated compulsion. No one else to blame but me for having unleashed this nasty woman from inside myself. Clearly I had no control over her aims. She would not be reeled in, so I guessed I had no choice. I had to.

I yanked his hand out from inside me, grabbed the extra tubing coming off my IV, and wrapped it around his wrist a few times. Having used up practically all the slack, he had no choice but to keep his hand adjacent to mine.

Heightening the stakes, I instructed him, as if he wasn't already all too aware, "If you make one false move, *cariño*, you'll tear this IV from my wrist and blood will spatter all over your hands." *I've always had a thing for literal figures of speech.*

I guided our hands back under the covers, to where I needed them most, hovering just above so as to draw out the torture for both Gabriel and me. He was panting with want, I was aching with need. Curling my pinky and ring fingers around his, I shoved both sets of our first two fingers inside me deeply. Four fingers filled me beautifully. I held us there and could feel the strange sensation of my pussy quivering around both of us at the same time. It all lent itself to the dreamlike quality of the situation I'd somehow managed to get myself into.

Gabriel grew impatient and began pushing in even deeper and so I pulled him out almost completely, granting only our fingertips the gift of lingering inside me for moments that stretched on like days. Having taught him his lesson, I thrust us back inside of me and then immediately forced us out. Our fingers in tandem, fucking me in and out, as fast as my risky bondage would allow. I slammed my hungry cunt down on us just one more time, shuttering and burying us deep inside before curling our fingertips onto my G-spot. I was so close to coming, my body writhing against the once-sterile sheets, it only took a few flicks to push me over the edge. I was weightless, spiraling in slow motion; my head hit the glass and I heard it shatter as my body quaked and I spurted all over our hands.

I opened my eyes and yet again Gabriel met me with his invading gaze, this time just inches from my face. Suddenly, he rammed his tongue into my mouth and we delighted in tasting each other—sucking, biting, wrestling back and forth, tongues snaking around each other, sliding in and out of each other's mouths. Finally we broke away, heaving air into our emptied lungs. His piercing eyes radiated pure temptation.

He leaned in and kissed my forehead with the longing of insatiability, the tender sweetness of a fallen angel. "I'm going to give you something to help you sleep through the night."

I began to protest, but he wouldn't hear of it. Gabriel grinned at me lasciviously. "With all that blood we got pumping inside you, your head is going to start pounding any minute now... Just as soon as the pounding in your pussy wears off."

So I acquiesced and felt my eyelids start to flutter almost instantaneously, heavy with the swirling of dreams. Willing them not to close so that my eyes could savor him just a little longer, I leaned forward slightly and this time he took my hand. *"Gracias, angelita.* This was definitely one hell of an unexpected...and delicious...send-off. Any time I feel a pang of loneliness in Aracataca, I'll take myself back to this moment and revel in tonight." Gabriel kissed me just once more with lust on his breath, crossed the room and looked back at me as I was already drifting off. He closed the door behind him, whispering, *"Que sueñes con los angelitos."* And I could feel my dreams cascading over me before I even heard the door click shut.

I slowly wake. A smile creeps across my face before I bother to think of opening my eyes, the early dawn just barely edging out the night. Luxuriating in this sensuous feeling, I give myself a minute to bask in the glow of the previous night before welcoming the break of daylight. I squeeze my eyes shut tightly, my cheeks already flushed with the thought of how I can prove to myself that last night's thrills were not a dream. I bring my fingers to my face and inhale. Yes, last night was definitely real. An incredibly hot send-off on a long journey for him, a much briefer one for me. Today I get discharged from Misericordia, my head suddenly feeling perfectly clear. The excitement at being able to go home to my own bed and real life again washes over my pleasurable memories.

Not wanting to watch the clock, I think up an ingenious way to pass the time. I decide to do something I've never done before—fill out a comment card. They ask you to offer praise or helpful suggestions, so why wouldn't I bestow accolades upon the most praiseworthy nurse I had ever had the pleasure of attending me? Using disguised language, I lay out the details that made my stay at Misericordia unlike any other: Gabriel's personal touch, his attention to detail, how he went above and beyond, even his meticulousness with my IV—they all are given the proper acknowledgment that they deserve. I grin as I write out the last line: *He seems bound for success.* Noting one blank spot on the card, I set out for the nurse's station. He may never know the extent of my gratitude, but at least I would have the satisfaction of putting it out there.

I ask the head nurse for Gabriel's last name and she stares at me quizzically, cocking her head just slightly. "I'm sorry, miss,

I've been here a long time and as far back as I can recall, we've never had a nurse, or anyone actually, employed in this hospital by that name."

A flash of pain darts across my vision as my memories start to spiral. Reality slides out from under me, twisting in slow motion, sending everything around me spinning.

ROPE DROUGHT

Teresa Noelle Roberts

R ain on the roof of the farmhouse woke them, the soft drumming alien after six rainless weeks. The sound infiltrated
slowly, filling Ellie's senses, filling a body that had felt as parched
as their fields and pastures until she felt compelled to spring
from bed, shut off the ancient, struggling air conditioner and
fling open the other windows to let in the earthy, damp breeze.
Energy zinged through her. She'd never thought of rain on the
roof as an erotic sound, but to a farmer, after a drought, each
drop that shushed on the roof sounded like a sigh of pleasure.
She could imagine the rain as a thousand hands, caressing their
crops and pastures—caressing her and Zeke too. Silly, maybe,
but the image excited her, or maybe it was just the sheer animal
joy of moisture in the air at last. "Come on!" she urged until
Zeke followed her lead, going from room to room until every
window and door in the old farmhouse was open to the night
and the rain.

They stood on the back porch, naked and finally, blessedly,

not overheated, watching the rain as it fell in slow, steady sheets, illuminated by the porch light. "The Weather Channel said that if this front reached us and didn't pass right over, it should rain on and off all week. Too bad there's no thunder," Ellie whispered, cuddling close to Zeke. "Lightning and thunder would make it perfect."

Zeke kissed the top of her head. "I know you love your thunderstorms, but this is the kind of rain we need." Unlike Ellie, Zeke had been raised on a farm, and he knew in his bones all the things Ellie was trying to learn from reading and talking to the neighbors, who were both amused by and supportive of their efforts to turn the failed dairy farm into a mixed-used organic farm, with vegetables and humanely raised meat.

Zeke pulled her close, as if relieved the cool breeze finally allowed it. "Quiet rain's steady," he explained. "Big flash-bangs don't last long. Rain comes down too hard, too fast and most of it just runs off. This isn't as dramatic but should go until morning before it tapers off."

"Like you." She grinned at him and saw his answering smile, bright against his tanned face even in the dark. Her farmer wasn't flashy, wasn't loud, but boy could he go on until morning.

That is, he could when they weren't both too stressed by the lack of rain that pushed their makeshift irrigation setup past its limits (who ever thought you'd need to irrigate in central New York, where too much rain was the more usual problem?); the crisp, browning grass in pastures that should have been lush for their young beef cattle; the knowledge that all the farms around them were just as bad off, so hay, if anyone had it to spare, would be expensive; the nasty choice they might soon face of slaughtering early or switching to corn feed, an added expense that would lower the price and quality of what they'd hoped would be the grass-fed beef that commanded a premium price in city markets. And feed corn mostly came from the Midwest, where the drought was far worse. It was only their second year on the farm, and even if the weather had been perfect, they'd have been struggling some. Farming was never easy and they had a lot to learn, even Zeke. But the drought made everything hard and frightening.

It had been a long dry summer in a lot of ways. But now that the weather had broken, maybe the sex-drought could break as well. Ellie felt Zeke's cock stirring against her, as he, too, experienced the sound of the rain, the rain-wet wind, as wild, damp caresses.

"Let's go for a walk," Ellie tugged on his arm.

"We're naked." He sounded amused.

"I know. Won't the rain feel nice on your skin?"

She danced out of his arms, danced off the porch and spun around on the little path through the herb-and-flower garden, sad and wilted, but starting to perk up a bit in the rain. "It's so warm and silky!" She began to laugh, softly at first, then bubbling out loud and clear. There were no neighbors to disturb, just like there were no neighbors to see them cavorting around naked. It was one of the attractions of this particular farm, one of the reasons they'd chosen it. Farming was hard work, but Ellie and Zeke had hoped they'd be able to play as hard as they worked—and they didn't like their play confined to a bedroom any more than they liked their work confined to an office.

Zeke stepped off the porch. "God, this feels good."

"I feel like a plant, like I've been dry so long I need to stay out here and soak up the rain."

All lean muscle and slick skin and hard cock, Zeke caught her in his arms and kissed her. As she relaxed into the kiss, into the wonder of his body in the soft, necessary rain, he grabbed her wrists and brought her arms together behind her back, where he could clasp both wrists with one big hand. "I know what you need," he whispered, pausing to lick water droplets off her ear. "What I need, too. I need to take you hard, out here."

"Honoring the rain." Ellie writhed against him. "Like some ancient pagan ritual."

"If outdoor sex makes it keep raining, why not?" He bent his head to suckle her nipple. His mouth was hot, ravenous, and the way her arms were trapped—the way *she* was trapped by his wiry farmer's strength—went right to her cunt. She moaned as she moved to straddle his thigh, grinding herself against him, leaving a hotter, slicker trail on his already moist, damp skin.

"Behave!" He smacked her ass with his free hand. She giggled and stuck her butt out, wiggling, which encouraged him to smack her a few more glorious times in rapid succession.

How long had it been since he'd spanked her? Too long, long enough that she jumped away from the sting, so much sharper than it used to be when they were playing regularly, before the rain stopped falling and the fear closed in. As soon as she jumped away, though, she pressed back toward his hand and begged, "Please..."

"Please what?" Zeke liked that game, liked to take advantage of those times when her talkative, English-major side was derailed by lust so she could answer only words of one syllable. She hadn't quite reached that point yet, but the reminder of what she'd been missing was pushing her in that direction. Luckily, she needed only words of one syllable.

"Tie me up and spank me. It's been too long."

He pulled her even closer. "Do you want to go inside? That's where the toys are, and the rope."

As the rain washed away the dry, sad weeks, Ellie whispered, "No. Out here."

Zeke's grin lit up the night. "I'll be right back," he said. He ran his hands down her back, stroking her ass, caressing around her body to glide over her slick belly and breasts. His hands left tingling trails behind, and she shuddered with pleasure. Then he returned to her wrists, still resting on top of each other behind her back, where he had left them. He gripped them, his touch fierce and demanding, in a way it hadn't been for a time. "Don't move. That's an order. I'll be right back." He kissed her, a deep kiss that promised much, and headed inside.

As he loped into the house she left her face up to the sky, her mouth open, greeting the rain as it fell. Kissing it as it kissed her.

Zeke was back before she had time to miss him, carrying a battery lantern, its yellow light contained by rainfall, and some soft rope, a spare length of cotton clothesline that lived in a kitchen drawer. He shifted her hands in front of her, tied them together quickly. It was the simplest of ties, little more than a loop, but for Ellie, bondage had never really been about elaborate ropework and strange positions. No, it was the soft, firm touch of the rope that did her in, and the sense of being, for the time she was bound, Zeke's possession, though at all other times they were equals. Because this tie was so simple Zeke could do it without a second thought, because within seconds he was leading her by the rope away from the house, it added to the illusion that she was a possession. A slave. A pagan sacrifice.

In the other hours of the day, she'd smack Zeke if he even hinted he thought of her that way, but now the fantasy made her tremble, slicked her thighs with her own hot moisture on top of the cooling rainwater.

Zeke led her to the poles that held the clothesline, hung the lantern on the crosspiece. It hung at a slight angle, so the circle of light it cast on the browned-out grass was asymmetrical. For some reason, Ellie's brain clung to that detail as Zeke untied her wrists, then positioned her so he could tie one wrist to each

side of the A-frame that supported the clothesline. He'd cut
the rope into shorter lengths, she realized. Probably used her
kitchen shears, a homely detail that cut through the fantasy of
being a slave staked out for punishment, or as a sacrifice to the
gods of rain.

The reality made it more erotic, rather than less so. He had
only enough rope to loop around one of her ankles and tether
it to the post, more a symbol than a real restraint, yet that too
seemed hot. So much of their life on the farm was like this,
makeshift, making do with what they had. But they had each
other, and now they had rain, so it was all right. Perfect, even.

And the warm rain was still coming down, drenching her,
drenching Zeke, soaking into the ropes. The ropes were cotton,
so as they got wet, they'd stretch to the point where the bondage
would be even more symbolic. She didn't care. Sometimes the
symbol was all she needed.

Zeke adjusted the lantern on its makeshift hook—so the light
fell better on her ass, she speculated—then got into position
himself, lining up to spank her. Tingling and throbbing with
anticipation Ellie thrust her ass out before she was told, pulling
on her bonds just for the pleasure of feeling that long-missed
tug, that tug that pulled intangibly on her nipples and clit.

The first spank felt like thunder, felt like the sky opening. She
rebounded back from Zeke's hand and yelped, even though she
repositioned herself immediately, eager for more spanking. And
more came, that wonderful combination of sting and seduction,
soaring pleasure and the safe confines of rope. After the first
few smacks, she stopped trying to count—it was all so surreal
tied up in the drenched dark that counting anything, even the
number of times she was spanked, seemed as futile as counting
raindrops. Better just to experience the spanking, soak it in
as the parched ground soaked in the rain. Her ass throbbed,

and her cunt throbbed along with it, open and hot and slick. Her butt felt huge, and so did her clit. Even the slightest movement magnified the sensation of the wet rope. Each raindrop that danced over her nipple or slipped into the crack of her ass aroused her more. Her world narrowed to rope and rain and Zeke's hand inflaming her, turning water to steam and restraint to freedom.

As they played, the rain picked up, washing over them like a great, warm wave, isolating Ellie even further from what might pass as reality. Was the house still there? Did she even care? Lost in sensation, she had trouble comprehending when Zeke said, "The way you've stuck your ass out, you have a puddle at the base of your spine." She couldn't imagine what he meant until he bent over and licked rainwater out of the hollow of her arched back.

She shuddered and mewled. The rain was warm and so was the air, but in comparison, Zeke's tongue was shockingly hot as he licked and kissed up her spine. His cock pressed against her, seeking entrance. She widened her stance, and the movement reminded her how her ankle was secured, though Zeke had left plenty of play in that tether. Zeke whispered something else, but it was lost behind rain and the blood rushing to her head. "Yes," she moaned, though she didn't know what question she answered.

Zeke knew what she meant, though. Zeke always knew, even if she didn't know herself. He entered her, driving hard, like the rain drove into the earth, his hands clasping her hips, pulling her back against him so while he took her, she was taking him. Each thrust moved her so she felt the ropes again, reminded her that she was tied. Each thrust splashed rainwater as the warm deluge sluiced over them. Fire shot through her, countering all that water, balancing it. She swore her skin steamed. Her cunt clasped on

Zeke's cock, so solid amid all the water. Rain and rope, rope and rain, and Zeke's strength, Zeke's persistence, Zeke's determination that had kept the farm and Ellie going during the drought and now was turned to their mutual pleasure.

Zeke slid one hand from her hip to her clit, wet fingers spiraling on that even slicker nub.

Ellie detonated so hard she thought briefly the light behind her eyelids was lightning, thought the explosion in her pussy and her blood might be thunder. But lightning ended almost instantly, and thunder rumbled for only a few seconds. This bright roar went on and on, as her body burst apart into light and reformed over and over again on the centering points of rope and cock and the rain that reminded her of the outlines of her skin, the edges, now blurred, that separated her from Zeke. She was crying out, not Zeke's name or even "Oh, god," but strange, guttural cries that didn't seem so strange against the drumming of the rain, and her body was trembling, and still, she was coming.

Just when she thought it was over, like a violent but brief cloudburst, Zeke surged into her. His grip tightened, though his fingers scrambled a bit for purchase on her wet skin. Zeke was a quiet comer but the force of this orgasm shook Ellie and set her off again.

Before he untied her, Zeke gently pushed Ellie's sodden hair off her face, gave her a soft kiss.

"Still raining," he whispered. "Looks like the drought's really broken."

"It sure has." Half-dazed as she was, Ellie still managed to grin.

JUSTICE

Sadey Quinn

Y ou put money in, and you choose a setting," he explained, sliding a crisp ten-dollar bill into the machine.

I kept my eyes on her as he fiddled with the controls. She was bound to a metal stool by thick, white straps. Her arms and legs were spread and tied to the ceiling and floor, respectively. Her jet-black hair was damp with sweat, clinging to her shoulders. Mascara ran a little around her eyes and looked sexy as hell. I wanted to touch her but there were two panes of glass between us and her naked body. I couldn't help but imagine it was me, not her, tied to the machine.

She lit up, like she'd been shocked, and let out a low, steady moan. I turned to him. "What'd you do?"

"She has a plug in her ass," he explained. "And one in her pussy. That white piece of fabric, right there?" He pointed to her cunt and I nodded; I saw it. "That's right on her clit. There's clear tape holding electrodes against her nipples, too."

I surveyed her body and saw the very faint lines of the

edges of the tape. She shivered and convulsed slightly. Her eyes glazed over and a faint smile crossed her lips before she sighed happily.

"So, I paid for her to feel intermittent vibration in her ass for the next five minutes. You want to try?"

He stepped aside and pointed to the controls. I shrugged, and dug into my pocket for a ten. I slid it in, but it was rejected, crinkled and used compared to his. Trying again, it went in, and I looked down at the panel.

"I can spank her?" I asked.

He grinned. "*You* can't. But you can direct it. Press the button and a number. You can do up to seven for ten dollars. Twenty, with twenty bucks."

I nearly rolled my eyes at the absurdity of it all, but obediently pressed the button, then chose THREE. I watched as the machine forcibly bent her forward, the straps holding her arms and legs supporting her weight. The plug went with her, and I clenched my own asscheeks, imagining how uncomfortable it would be to be spanked with a butt plug inside me. Her eyes looked out at us, and though I knew she couldn't see us through the one-sided glass, she did know we were there. Watching her. Coordinating her torture. She looked worried and I couldn't blame her.

A metal robotic arm appeared from the right wall and magnetically picked up a long wooden paddle with a metal handle. The woman cringed in anticipation.

"Does she know how many she'll get?" I asked.

"Nope."

"She seems scared."

"Rightfully so."

I shot a sideways glance in his direction. He stared forward, sadistically entranced by the scene.

The robotic arm brought the paddle down once, *hard*, against her bubbly posterior. I watched through the mirrored walls as her flesh moved around the impact of that paddle, as she shook her cute little ass, and then we both jumped slightly when we heard her cry out.

"Oh! Fuck!"

Once more, the paddle swatted her butt.

"No! Oh, please!"

Who was she begging, exactly?

And the third time, the sound of the wood against her skin reverberating through the observation area. Her moans followed.

"Intensity goes up?" I asked, watching as she was maneuvered back into position on the stool.

"Yeah. You have money left."

He was eager for more, but I was eager to prolong things for my sake and hers. I looked behind me and saw the line was even longer.

"They'll all take a turn with her?"

"No. Check the clock, see?" He pointed to a digital timer just above the control kiosk. "Forty minutes left. Then the next convict gets a turn."

Surveying the options in front of me, I chose what I'd be desperate for, if I were in her shoes. Three-minute vibration on her clitoris.

He chuckled beside me, shaking his head. "You're evil."

I looked at him quizzically, then cringed as the woman screamed.

"No!" she shouted, convulsing against the bondage, clearly trying to get away.

"I thought she would enjoy it," I gasped.

In under thirty seconds, she came fast, forcibly, and whimpered loudly as the buzzing continued.

"No...no...no..." she kept saying.

God, she was so fucking hot.

He slipped an arm around my waist and pulled me close as we watched her come again, her body trembling, her moans and pleas never ending.

"How many times do you think she's come today?" he asked.

I shook my head. My breathing was shallow and at that moment I wanted nothing more than to switch places with her, to be tortured so terribly. So sexually.

By the time the buzzing stopped, she'd come four times. We stepped aside and the next person, a stout bald man with a thick wallet, stepped forward and slipped in a fifty-dollar bill. I wanted to stay and watch her torment but he pulled me away, up the stairs and out to the street.

"Can't we go back and watch more?" I asked, shielding my eyes from the light.

"No."

I pretended to pout and he pulled me toward him, grabbing my ass hard, and looked down into my eyes. "That was fore-play, babe." He kissed me urgently and my knees buckled. I grasped his shoulders for support.

"You'll do things to me...things like that?" I whispered as he broke away and tugged me toward his car.

He only smiled and opened the passenger door. "Get in. We're going to my place."

DARKNESS
AND LIGHT

Sophia Valenti

Dana couldn't understand why I'd dumped Roger. The breakup had happened last month, but she still couldn't let it go.

"He's the perfect guy!" she exclaimed. "The total package."

I wasn't going to try to explain myself—again. But for some reason, that most likely being the tequila, I started to speak.

"That all depends on what your idea of the total package is." Dana cocked her head, looking a little drunk and a lot confused. "Sure, he was handsome and sweet—"

"And what's wrong with that!"

"He was too...nice." The word hung in the air, only adding to her confusion. But I wasn't referring to the fact that Roger always held the door and paid for dinner. I was talking about the polite missionary-position sex he favored, and that I did not.

I looked at my friend, who was the epitome of vanilla. Sure, she and I had dished about our dates, but always in the most general terms, like if a guy was good in bed. We'd never defined "good," but I knew what my version of good meant: someone who was very, very bad—a guy who'd take me to dark, sexy places where I could leave every earthly care behind. Once upon a time, I'd hoped that would be Roger, but I learned soon enough that wasn't the case.

One night, after he'd asked what he could do for me in bed, I'd suggested that we try something more daring. He looked as confused as Dana did now, and when I started to talk about handcuffs and blindfolds, he shut me down. We weren't the type of people who did *those* things, he told me. I stopped speaking; there was nothing left to say. Because deep down I knew I was one of those people, and he clearly was not.

That was the beginning of the end.

The end of the end came after my first night with Graham, a man who was as affectionate as I could have ever hoped for, yet was as intensely dominant as I craved. I was never one to dream of white knights. The dark ones were the only sort that had ever invaded my fantasies, and Graham fit that description to a T.

I realized that Dana was still staring at me, her big blue eyes searching for an answer.

"I just liked things that Roger didn't," I offered as an explanation, hoping that would be enough to satisfy her, but it wasn't.

"Like what?"

Figuring she was too drunk to judge—and probably too drunk to remember what I'd say—I didn't hold back.

"Like being bound and blindfolded." I felt my cheeks go hot.

Fortunately, Dana seemed more confused than offended. "I don't know why anyone would want to be blindfolded," she said with a shake of her head, making her blonde curls bounce around her face. "I mean, when it's dark, all you see is nothing!"

Nothing? I opened my mouth to answer, but I stopped

myself. I knew she'd never understand, and in an instant, my mind drifted back to that night with Graham—the night that changed everything.

I work in public relations, and while many of my fellow journalism school graduates scoff at the notion, I love it. I like meeting new people, making connections and spreading the word about people and things I'm passionate about. The agency had been pretty traditional, however, and the owner recently decided we needed to move into the twenty-first century. While we had a fabulous client list, we were quaint and old-fashioned in that we were neglecting the potential of social media, which is why my boss hired Graham as a consultant.

I was looking forward to hearing what advice he had for us, but my expectations ended there. I will admit that I had a preconceived notion of who would show up at my office. I was expecting a scruffy twentysomething who was fresh out of college. Graham was nothing of the sort, but there was indeed much he had to teach me.

Tall and broad, Graham looked stunning in his exquisitely tailored suit. With his dark eyes and wavy black hair, he looked more like an action-movie hero than an executive. During our first meeting, he laid out his roadmap for implementing social-media strategies, and I was impressed with his thorough proposal and sensible advice. He was charismatic and personable, his take-charge nature buoyed by his confidence and intelligence. I felt drawn to him in a way I'd never before been to another man.

Graham and I worked together closely over the next two weeks, and while the days flew by, my nights were slow to pass. I'd lie wide-awake on the pristine white cotton sheets that Roger favored as my mind wandered into dangerous territory. I'd recall

Graham's muscular body, so temptingly close to mine as he stood behind me and leaned over my shoulder to point out something on my computer screen. The way his deep brown eyes would linger on me a second too long made me wonder if he was having the same late-night fantasies that I was—ones that involved Graham taking control of me, and delivering whatever pleasure or pain he thought I deserved. I pictured him using his colorful silk neckties to bind me facedown on his bed, pulling his thick leather belt out of its loops, and making me beg to be punished.

I wanted it—I wanted it all. To be bound and blindfolded and whipped until I came. I was scared and nervous, and incredibly aroused. Just thinking about it was enough to make my pussy flood. I also felt guilty, like I'd somehow cheated on Roger when all I'd done was let my sleep-deprived mind run free. But not so guilty that I didn't reach a hand inside my panties, find the swollen knob of my clit and rub myself until I climaxed, all the while thinking of Graham.

I tried to tell myself that these were just crazy dreams, that I was merely inserting Graham into these scenarios because he and I were spending so much time together. But they weren't dreams, and I wasn't asleep—though I realized I'd been going through the motions in my daily life as though I were. There had to be more, and that didn't involve settling for someone who couldn't accept me for who I was.

As the days had passed, the easygoing rapport I had with Graham had been edging ever closer to outright flirtation. I found myself admiring his fit figure, my mind tumbling into intermittent fantasies about him pressing me up against a wall and having his way with me. When I thought he wasn't looking, I'd let my gaze drop to the leather belt at his waist. It looked thick and supple, and to anyone else it was simply a fashion accessory. But thanks to my filthy dreams, it was so much more.

By his last day at work, that little spark between us was ready to flare into an out-of-control inferno.

At five o'clock, Graham switched off his laptop, declaring me ready to take the reins. I smiled, but inside I was conflicted. I didn't want him to leave.

As if he heard my thoughts, Graham reached out and took my hand in his.

"Although my contract is up, I don't think my work here is done." Graham stroked his thumb along the back of my hand as he spoke, and I felt tingles shoot straight to my cunt. The implication of his unsaid words sent delicious shivers through my body.

"What do you mean?"

"Have dinner with me." It wasn't a question. It was more like a declaration of fact.

I called Roger to let him know I'd be working late. He didn't seem to mind. After all, he reminded me, he had to turn in early to make his eight a.m. tee-time at the club.

Graham escorted me out of the office building with a possessive hand on the small of my back. I could feel the heat of his palm through the fabric of my dress. The sensation made me long to feel his flesh against my own. He'd yet to say anything sexual, but it was clear from the beginning where the night would end—in his apartment, in his bed.

Graham hailed us a cab, directing the driver to bring us to a trendy restaurant I'd seen mentioned in the gossip pages but at which I had never dined. After an effusive greeting from the hostess, we were whisked away to a small private dining room, where Graham ordered for both of us. I let him. I liked that he seemed set on taking care of every last detail, on taking care of me. I wanted that. It seemed like I spent so much of my days working on everyone else's behalf. I reveled in the notion that

I could simply stop and be nothing but the object of one handsome man's total attention.

The dinner was decadent and rich. Graham took every opportunity to hold my hand or stroke my cheek. I barely touched my wine; I was already dizzy with lust from being in such an intimate setting with the object of my fantasies.

"Now that we're no longer working together, I feel I can be more honest," Graham said, his voice having taken on a slightly husky tone.

"About what?"

"About how much I want you."

I looked away, feeling shy and overwhelmed.

"I have a boyfriend," I said unconvincingly.

"But he's not enough for you—otherwise you wouldn't be here with me."

Graham was right, and that's why I went home with him.

He was on me the second his door shut. Grabbing the back of my head, Graham tangled his fingers in my ebony curls and held me still for a brutally intense kiss. He fisted the hair at the nape of my neck and gave it a tug, sparking a flash of pain that made me gasp into his open mouth. He thrust his tongue between my parted lips, claiming me with his kiss, keeping me breathless and on edge as he walked me backward toward his bedroom.

Swiftly and efficiently, Graham stripped me of my work clothes, until there was nothing left for me to hide behind.

The look of raw hunger on his face made my pussy pulse. I felt truly wanted for the first time in my life. My heart was beating wildly and adrenaline rushed through my veins, but there was no place I'd rather have been.

Still fully clothed, Graham took my naked body in his arms, pulling me close for another deep kiss that tasted of whiskey and was laced with dirty promises. He traced his fingers down my arms, ending at my wrists, which he pulled behind my back and held fast with one big hand. I squirmed against him, feeling trapped and thrilled all at once.

Graham trailed his lips along my jawline, the rasp of his stubble causing my skin to pebble with goose bumps.

"You like this," he hissed in my ear. "I can tell. You like being at my mercy."

Graham nipped at the tender skin of my neck, and I moaned softly as his free hand stroked my bare ass.

"That's what I like to hear, darlin'. You're going to look so sweet tied down to my bed."

My loud gasp gave away all my secrets. But even if I hadn't uttered a sound, Graham's fingers slipping between my parted thighs easily determined my truth. My pussy was wet and slick, dripping at the thought of being made his captive, of having every one of my filthy fantasies become pulse-quickening realities. My knees felt weak as Graham stroked his fingers along my slit, picking up my moisture and smearing it over my swollen clit. His slow, sexy circles teased me as he continued to croon, "You want it bad, don't you, Josie?"

I let out another moan that was cut short by a hard slap to my ass.

"Answer me when I ask you a question," he insisted.

"Y-yes, I want it," I managed to reply.

"Want what, baby?"

Oh, god. Don't make me say it.

Another harsh slap on the other cheek encouraged me to find my voice.

"I want you to tie me down, to blindfold me," I whispered, eyes downcast. In a way, this conversation was more difficult than the one I'd had with Roger. Probably because I knew Graham would follow through.

"And what else?" he asked, his voice warm and smooth—he was the devil in a pinstriped suit. His fingers flitted across my bare ass again, and I found myself not wanting to hold back any longer, even though the thought of admitting my desires terrified me.

"And then I want you to punish me—with your belt," I uttered in a hushed whisper.

"Jesus, Josie, you're even dirtier than I'd hoped." His voice was heavy with lustful admiration.

Graham released my hands and stepped back. I looked up and saw him gazing at me hungrily as he loosened his necktie.

"Eyes closed," he said softly, before wrapping his red silk tie around my head and tying it snugly.

I found comfort in the darkness. It let me escape from the world and focus on nothing but the desire within me.

Graham helped me up onto the bed, wordlessly laying me down on my stomach. I stretched out against the cool sheets, my body limp with surrender as I let him position me how he wanted. I felt more soft fabric being wrapped around my wrists as they were tied together; he must have attached my bonds to his headboard because when I tugged my hands, I felt resistance. I heard the swish of his belt being pulled out of its loops—just like I'd imagined in my fantasy—and my skin prickled with fear as I realized I couldn't get away.

"Your ass is going to look so pretty after it's been striped by my belt."

A split second later, I felt the leather snap against my skin. The spark of pain cleared my head, and I groaned into the mattress. Graham didn't give me a chance to fully absorb the belt's impact before landing another blow. I arched my back and raised my hips as the pain blossomed into heat that spread to my cunt and made me ache even more for him.

My hands balled into fists as I pulled and tugged, but the bonds held me fast. Meanwhile Graham's unforgiving belt laid down layer after layer of heat, crisscrossing my ass and thighs. My cries of abandon were interspersed with whimpers of longing as I felt myself growing increasingly aroused.

After a dozen strokes of the belt, I was squirming wildly on the bed, tilting my hips toward the sheets and trying to give my clit the friction it needed. In the haze of my lust, I heard Graham chuckle softly and say, "Such a greedy little slut."

Still surrounded by darkness, I focused on what little cues I could hear and feel: the rustle of Graham stripping out of the rest of his clothes and the pitch of the mattress as he climbed onto the bed with me. I arched my back as he palmed my heated cheeks, lewdly exposing me. But I was too turned on to be embarrassed. Graham groaned into my slick flesh as he tricked his tongue along my dripping slit and discovered how wet I was. I squirmed against his face, so hot and ready to come, and Graham indulged my desire. Locking his lips around my clit, he swirled his tongue around that puffy button, sucking and licking until my body stiffened with pleasure.

I was still crying out from my sudden and overwhelming climax as Graham rose and shoved his cock into my quivering sex. With bold, forceful strokes, he rode me toward another climax, which soon triggered his own.

Afterward, Graham loosened my bonds and removed the blindfold, holding me possessively in his arms. And just like that my world had changed. But I guess, in reality, it was simply that I had changed.

All you see is nothing. Dana's false words echoed in my head. I could never explain it to her in a way she could understand.

Rather than nothing, I'd seen sparks of red and gold shimmer against my eyelids as bursts of pleasure lit me up from the inside. I'd seen the fulfillment of so many years of fevered dreams. And I'd seen what my future could be and knew that there was no way I would ever go back to the way things were.

Nothing? No, I'd seen everything.

BROKEN

Alison Tyler

Lifeguards can stay young forever.

Dean didn't want to grow up. He coasted in the type of lifestyle that fit his immature personality. He worked the pool circuit—the country club, the park rec—and he spent his free time at the gym. Staying young. He had sandy blond hair that he wore thick and slightly shaggy. His muscles were more intense than when he'd been in his twenties. At home, he had posters on his walls, even though most of his friends had traded up to framed artwork. There was something college boy about every aspect of his life. That's how he liked it.

And each year, he went to Spring Break.

"Can't believe you're still heading to Florida," his friend Tommy said. "You're twenty years older than all the bikini babes."

Dean looked at himself in the mirror behind the bar. Did he look forty? He didn't think so. Maybe there were a few creases around the corners of his eyes, but that's what sunglasses were for.

"I can do two hundred crunches a day," Dean said.

"Fine," Tommy responded. "But how much you got in your 401(k)?"

A long time ago, Tommy had been fun. Around the frat house, they'd had good times with lots of broads. Now Tommy was married with a mortgage and a wife named Susan who didn't like Dean. She was still pissed about the bachelor party, and that was what? Seven years ago? Tommy had to lie to see Dean, meeting after work at a pub. Dean swore he'd never hook up with a woman who kept him away from his friends.

"Our buddies are all getting married," Tommy told him. "Look around, man. The group has grown up. You're like one of the fucking Lost Boys."

Dean took that as a compliment. He let Tommy pay, because Tommy had the cash, and then he said, "I'll call you when I get back from Miami." He knew that somewhere deep inside, his friend was jealous. Wouldn't Tommy like to pack his swimming trunks and favorite tees and go for a week to a place with no worries? In Miami, you could make eye contact with a pretty bikini and be in bed with her in less then fifteen minutes. And then you could go back out into the lavender evening and meet up with another girl, even prettier than the first, and do the same thing all over again. As long as you could get your dick hard, you could find some warm, wet place to stick it in.

The flight was actually one of Dean's favorite parts of Spring Break, because the anticipation by this point was almost over-powering. He flirted with the stewardesses, almost randomly. One seemed interested in him, and he had the inclination to tell her, *Sorry sweetheart, you're too old for me.* He was looking for those hard bodies in the thongs and the tiny triangles, looking for the bars on the beach where a sarong was overkill. But he played the lothario until landing, and when the flight attendant gave him her number, he took it and winked. She didn't see him toss the paper into the garbage as he exited the chilled airport into the muggy heat of Florida.

He was staying at an old college buddy's house to save money. 401K, my ass. He spent what he brought in, saving only enough to splurge on this one vacation every year. Brad was out of town, and Dean was supposed to have the place to himself. So when he turned the key in the lock and came face-to-face with a woman holding a baseball bat, he was beyond surprised.

"What the fuck?" they both said at the same time. Dean dropped his bag and put up his hands. He said, "I'm a friend of Brad's."

"How do I know that?"

"Would he tell me where the key was? How would I know to look under the potted chicken?"

The brunette stepped back but did not drop the Louisville Slugger.

"Look," he said, "I'll show you the letter from Brad. It's in my suitcase. We went to school together. I'm Dean."

"Dean." She squinted her eyes. He took the time to really look at her, summing her up the way he did all women, automatically. Tall and slim, about his age, good tits, very attractive actually if she would drop the fucking bat. He grabbed the letter from the pocket of his suitcase and showed it to her. She set the weapon down and then sat on the sofa.

"I'm sorry," she said. "I'm jumpy."

Yeah, clearly, he thought. *But who the fuck are you?*

She exhaled, seemingly defeated. "I've had a rough couple of nights," she said. "I just broke up with my boyfriend, and I had nowhere to go. Bradley said I could stay here. He must have forgotten to tell me that you were coming."

Dean kept quiet, watching as she poured some Jack Daniels

into what appeared to be a glass of lemonade, then thought better of it and drank from the bottle directly. After sipping, she handed the bottle to Dean. He took a sip gratefully and sat across from her in a wicker basket chair trying to calm down.

"Breakups suck," he said, although he didn't really mean it. He'd never experienced a painful breakup, hadn't ever dated long enough to care about anyone seriously.

"Yeah," she said. "And this was a big one. Ten years. A house." She put her hands to her face. Dean looked up at the mantel, and then he stood and walked over. There were pictures of this woman with Brad. Shit. She was obviously family.

"Are you one of Brad's sisters?" he asked the question tentatively, and she set her hands down and nodded.

"I'm Connie," she said.

"I went to college with Brad," he told her.

"You're *that* Dean?"

He didn't know what *that Dean* meant, but he nodded.

"You must want to unpack, take it easy." She looked like she felt bad she'd unloaded on him. He let her show him to the room he'd be staying in, the guest room in the two-bedroom bungalow. As he set his suitcase down, she said, "Would you like to go out later? Have dinner or a drink?"

No, he fucking wouldn't. He wanted to pick up some little chicklet and let her ride his cock all night long. Or at least half the night. He'd been waiting for this all fucking year. But this was Brad's sister, and she looked sad. He said, "Sure." He could always go out after.

Except, "after" didn't turn out the way he'd expected. They had dinner at a little seafood restaurant on the water, candles in lanterns making patterns on the table. Connie told him all about her ex, and what an asshole he'd been, and how she'd found him in bed with...wait for it...his fucking secretary. Dean inserted the different sighs and *oh nos* he felt were appropriate and he watched as she out drank him. He'd have her back at the pad in no time, still able to hit the clubs by midnight.

But when they got back to Brad's, Connie was clinging to him. "You're nice," she said. He wasn't. But alcohol will do that to you. "Take me to bed? It's been so long."

Jesus. Here was a girl offering it up to him. She was thirty-six, thirty-seven, about fifteen years past his internal expiration date, but she'd feel good to fuck. He could go out after, right? "Sure," he said again, his mantra for the evening.

Pity fuck or not, drunk or not, she was amazing in bed. She sucked his cock and looked up at him with her big, brown eyes. She rolled over and spread her legs and he gripped her hips and sunk inside her. Damn, that felt good. They both seemed to be sharing the thought at the same time. The look she shot him over her shoulder was pure bliss. He was certain his own expression echoed hers.

"This isn't how I usually like to fuck," she whispered.

"No? You like being on top?"

"Something like that. Maybe tomorrow."

But tomorrow he'd be banging the bikinis, he wanted to say. "Sounds good," was all he managed, as he touched her clit and felt her shiver beneath him. She came quietly; he followed a beat after. The dozed together for a little while, and when he woke up, she was asleep at his side. Perfect.

But when he tried to sneak out, she caught him at the front door. She didn't seem drunk at all now. "Where you going, Dean?"

"I was all hopped up," he said. "I thought I'd take my energy for a walk."

She had a white silk robe tight around her body. God, she was pretty. He didn't know what it was about her. The long black hair, full lips, the sad look in her eyes. He reached out and touched her face, and he felt a tightening in the pit of his stomach. The bikinis could wait until the morning. He returned to the bedroom with her, and he was surprised when she pushed him forcefully down on the bed.

"What we did before..." she started.

"Yeah?"

"That's not really my style."

He found himself interested. "What do you mean?"

She had cuffs in her hand, as if magically, and she dangled them in front of his face. "You want me to tie you to the bed?" he asked. He'd never played like that before.

"No," she said. "I want to tie *you* down."

His cock responded as if she'd spoken directly to it instead of to him. What was going on? He'd never even thought to do things kinky before. Most of the girls he dated were so young that simply the act of fucking was exciting to them.

"Are you game?" She put one hand on his dick. He was rock hard. "You seem game."

"I was going out," he said, to give himself a second to think.

She nodded. "I know. You were going out. Take off your shirt."

He could stop this charade at any second. He could tell her she was over the top, rebounding, using him to get her aggressions out. But he took off his shirt anyway. He was proud of his six-pack, of the rippling muscles of his arms and chest. She put one cuff on his left wrist. He didn't fight her. He could leave at any time, he told himself. She strung the chain through the headboard, and then put the cuff on his right wrist and clicked the lock shut. Dean tested his bindings, and realized that he'd have to take the bed with him now if he were going anywhere without her permission.

Connie continued, "You were going out, and then you were

going to pick up some little sunscreen-scented sophomore and screw her senseless."

Dean started to say, "No, no, I was just going to take a walk around the block. Clear my head..." but Connie put a hand to his mouth to quiet him.

She climbed on top of his body, her pussy to his cock through his pants, and he could feel her heat even through the layers of fabric. "And then you were going to go out again and pick up another one, a carbon copy, and fuck her just the same way. Does it ever get old for you, Dean?"

"How do you know all that about me?"

"You're Dean. You're legendary to Brad. He talks about you all the time. How you come out here every Spring Break. How you notch your belt with your kills."

In spite of himself, Dean was flattered. Brad had talked about him. Of their frat boy crew, Brad had been the shy one. Picking up girls had never come easy to him.

"You never stick around long enough to see whether you actually could like a girl or not, do you?"

"What's it to you?"

"Like, you don't even remember me."

He squinted at her. What was she talking about? "We just fucking met six hours ago."

She sighed and undid his shoes and pulled them off, then undid the buckle on his belt and pulled his slacks down. He felt odd to have a woman undress him, but his cock responded the way it had when she'd talked of tying him down. He could not remember ever being this excited before.

"You're as hot as you were in college," she said, and then he thought back. Graduation. The party. He would have been twenty-two, and Connie would have been eighteen. Constance. He saw the pert brunette in his mind, remembered fucking her in her parents' pool. Jesus, a lifetime ago.

"You were my first," she said. "You always remember your firsts."

He felt a pang. She hadn't been important to him at all. A number. A notch. A nobody he'd used, like he used all the others. What was Connie doing now? He watched as she pulled the belt free from his slacks. What was the point of that? His pants were already off. She snapped the leather, and the pang he'd felt a second before turned to anxiety. What was she going to do?

Connie bent and sucked his cock. He groaned and rattled the handcuff chain. Metal on metal. He begged her with his hips.

"We taste good together," she said. "I can taste my own juices on your cock."

The girls he dated never talked like that. They were cookie-cutter girls, all almost the same, like Barbies on a shelf. They let him fuck them. They let him use them. But they didn't talk like that.

"Now, roll over like a good boy."

"What the fuck?"

"Do it, Dean. You know you want to."

"What do I want? What do you think I want?"

She bent down and pressed her lips to the side of his neck and kissed him. Then she bit his left earlobe and whispered, "You want me to whip you, and then you want me to fuck you."

"You're crazy."

She put her hand on his cock. His dick throbbed.

"Am I?"

He swallowed and looked at her. "How do you know what I want?"

"Simple. Because you've been looking for years without ever finding it. Because you're on an endless quest, a nameless search, and you think you know what you're looking for...but you don't."

She climbed onto the mattress and got between his legs. She licked his balls and he rattled the headboard once more. Christ, what was she doing to him? His head was spinning.

"Turn over, Dean. Turn over and let me make it all better."

He could tell her to release him, and he was pretty sure she would. He thought he'd check to see.

"Undo the cuffs."

She pulled the key out immediately. It was dangling from a chain around her neck. "You want me to?" She moved to the headboard, but before she could insert the key into the lock, he stopped her.

"No." He'd just been testing. Now he saw that he was safe. If he needed her to let him go, she would. But he didn't want her to let him go. Not really.

He moved on the mattress, rolling over, the handcuff chain turning with him. He was stretched out on the bed on his stomach, his cock a living beast beneath him, craving release. He could feel the precome leaking out, and he wondered whether she knew how close he was.

She seemed to know everything.

Connie climbed off the bed and he turned to look at her. Stunning, that's what she was. In that white silk robe that barely skimmed her thighs, she was a vision. Her long hair was so perfectly pin-straight. Her eyes were bright and warm for being such a dark brown. He tended to do the blondes. But he suddenly couldn't remember why. She had small tits, and he always went for big knockers. She had slim hips, and that dark patch of curls between her thighs, and...

She doubled up the belt and then struck her first blow. He winced, but didn't say a word. His cock twitched. He would not say that he liked it, but he knew that he did. The pain turned something on inside of him, something he'd never felt before. She struck him again, and he bit the inside of his bottom lip. He wondered how hard she'd hit him, how long she'd make this last. The third blow made him exhale between his teeth, a hissing sigh. He knew all about pain from the gym. He worked out to the nth degree, keeping his body in the type of tip-top shape required for his extracurricular activities. He liked to push himself past his previous boundaries, always striving for a new level, a new number on the machines.

This pain was different. She hit him rapidly, crisscrossing his ass with the blows, and he saw red behind closed lids, a dark purply red that colored this new experience. Where there was pain, there was also pleasure. When she'd reached ten, Connie stroked her palm over his heated skin. She touched the welts, and he groaned.

"You like that." This wasn't a question.

He answered anyway, "Yeah." There was no reason to lie to her. She could tell for herself.

"You want to fuck me?" He looked at her, and he realized he did. Badly.

"Yeah."

"It will cost you ten more to fuck my pussy."

He nodded instantly. He could take ten more. She struck him, and she counted the blows. The leather seemed to lick at his skin, each stripe reverberating deep inside of him.

When she reached ten, he expected her to uncuff him, to let him at her, in her. He could not wait to feel her warm, wet pussy on his cock. But she paused and bent close to him once more, as she had at the start.

"You want me to fuck you?" she asked.

His heart pounded hard in his chest. What was she offering?

"Dean? You want me to fuck you?"

He nodded before he could stop himself, his head bobbing up and down.

"I'm sorry, Dean," she said, and she sounded genuinely sorry. "But it will cost you."

His ass was striped and hot. But he knew what she was going to say, and he knew his answer.

"Yeah," he said. "Yes. Whatever you want."

"It's about what you want. Don't you get that yet?"

He saw her at eighteen, in her parents' pool, that little scarlet bikini. How had he forgotten her? How had he blocked that night from his memory? Her hair had been shorter then, and her eyes hadn't seemed sad at all. They'd been hopeful. He'd felt pleased nailing such a pretty young thing, and doing it practically under the eyes of her rich daddy.

"I want it," he said. "Please. I want it."

"Ten more strokes," she told him. "You count this time."

He did, stuttering every few numbers, fucking the mattress with his hips when he couldn't help himself. She gave him an extra two for that. He was supposed to behave; she thought he understood.

When she reached twelve, she dropped the leather and went to her suitcase. He was shivering all over, watching as she brought out a harness and a dildo. She unzipped a little cosmetics case and drew out a bottle of lube. He felt her slick the liquid between his asscheeks, really working it into his hole with her pointer. He groaned and buried his face into the pillows. Embarrassment flooded through him, but when she slid one hand under his body and pumped his dick, he understood that she liked this as much as he did.

He watched her again, watched as she dropped the shorty robe and fastened on the harness and synthetic cock. She climbed onto the bed behind him, shoving him roughly into the position she wanted, splitting him open. There was more lube then, a river of lube, and he felt the slippery liquid dripping onto his balls.

"You remember fucking me that time, don't you?"

"Yeah."

"And the things you said to me?"

What had he said? Who remembered sex talk after eighteen years?

"You said I was beautiful."

"You were...you are..."

She had the head of the cock pressed right against his hole. He was tense with anticipation, waiting.

"You said you'd never been with a girl as pretty as me."

"I hadn't..." He didn't know what he was supposed to be saying. He was practically talking gibberish, waiting for her to push forward.

"And you took my number, but you never called."

He wanted to look at her, but she put one hand on the back of his head, pushing his face against the pillow. He couldn't meet her eyes, not from this position. He wanted to apologize for his former self, except his former self was who he was now. Who he'd always been. Tossing the numbers in the garbage, so many numbers, so many years.

"You're lucky," he said, turning his head so he was facing the wall. "You wouldn't have wanted to be with me."

That was true. He felt as if he was saying something honest. She slid the head of the cock into his ass, and he groaned and clenched his eyes shut tight. But somehow he couldn't stop talking.

"I was that guy," he panted. "The wrong guy. The one who only wanted to get in your pants. I've always been that guy."

She slid in deeper, and he groaned again. Christ, he'd never felt anything like that before.

"That's okay, Dean. You're forgiven. You took your punishment."

She was all the way in now, and he felt as if she was pounding into his soul. Her hips moved fast; she was really reaming him. His cock was a beast between his legs, demanding, wondering where the pussy was. His ass felt stuffed full, spread open. She pulled out, moving away from him, and he turned his head to look at her over his shoulder, desperate.

"Don't worry, Dean. I'm just adding more lube."

She patted him on the ass and then resumed the fucking. He never wanted it to stop. As she worked him now, she brought one hand under his body to jack his cock. Her fist was greasy from the lube, and he knew she was going to make him come.

"After I'm done, you can go out," she whispered. "You can go and get one of your little bikini babes. You can notch your belt."

"No," he shook his head. He'd almost reached his limits. "No, I won't. I don't want to."

"Why, Dean? Why not?"

He was panting, crazy with lust. "I want to stay here. With you."

"But I'll do cruel things to you."

Oh, god, she was going to make him spurt all over the white sheets.

"Tell me..." he was begging. "What will you do?"

"I'll make you eat me out for hours," she said. "I'll make you lick my asshole."

He was coming now, coming as she reamed his ass, coming all over her hand and the sheets and his belly. She pulled out and undid the harness, tossing the thing to the corner. She brought the handcuff key to the headboard and undid his left wrist. She pulled the cuffs free, but before she could undo his right wrist cuff, he clicked the left one back on. He was still her captive, simply not bound to the bed.

"Please," he said. He lay down on his back and he looked at her. "Let me."

"Let you what?"

"Sit on my face, Connie. Let me lick your pussy and your asshole. Don't set me free. I don't want to be free."

"Are you sure?" she asked. She squeezed his cock roughly as she spoke. He was already semihard again.

"Yes."

"How bad do you want it?"

His heart was a raging force in his chest. He had never felt like this before. Awake. Alive. Near desperate with need.

"It's all I want, Connie."

He had come to Spring Break, broken. He realized that as she positioned herself above him. He'd always been broken. She hovered over his face, teasing him, taunting him. He reared up, but she moved so she was out of reach.

"Please," he said, his voice husky with longing. "Please."

As he licked her ass, making tight circles with the point of his tongue, he realized that he'd changed. He was changing. No more Lost Boy for Dean. Connie arched her hips and spread her cheeks wide for him. He drove his tongue in her, thinking this was all he would ever want to do. He could move here. Be here with her. What better place for a lifeguard than Miami?

Connie fucked his face, and he swam in pleasure. He'd been broken, but she was fixing him. When she was done, he'd be glued together, maybe. Cracks and hair-fine fractures visible to anyone who knew where to look. But fixed, just the same.

He didn't want to be broken anymore.

TIE ME DOWN

Dan Grogan

I am the rope that binds you.
Restricting movement keeps you safe from dangers;
However you're relieved when you're let free.
Your blood and lymph flow normally again,
Mobility restored to aching limbs.
I'm lost now, though, just lying on the floor,
No longer having purpose, coiled
Upon myself and put away until
The next time I am needed to restrain you.
I know that someday I will be exhausted—
Frayed, kinked, broken—from efforts to confine,
And I will be discarded for new rope.

ABOUT THE
AUTHORS

By day, **JAX BAYNARD** is a financial investment advisor. By night, she makes her own (and her clients') fantasies come true. This part-time dominatrix's short fiction has appeared in *With This Ring, I Thee Bed*; *Pleasure Bound*; online and in several literary journals.

RACHEL KRAMER BUSSEL (rachelkramerbussel.com) is the editor of over fifty anthologies, including *Anything for You: Erotica for Kinky Couples, Spanked, Bottoms Up, Cheeky Spanking Stories, Orgasmic, Irresistible, Fast Girls* and is *Best Bondage Erotica* and *Best Sex Writing* series editor. She writes widely about sex, dating, books and pop culture.

Although **ANDREA DALE** sometimes dabbles in flash fiction, she doesn't necessarily believe that brevity is the soul of wit. Has she tantalized you? Do you want to know more? Visit cyvarwydd.com and see what else she has to say.

DANTE DAVIDSON's short stories have appeared in assorted anthologies including *Bondage; Naughty Stories from A to Z; Best Bondage Erotica; The Merry XXXmas Book of Erotica; Luscious; Morning, Noon, and Night* and *Sweet Life*. With Alison Tyler, he is the coauthor of the "classic" *Bondage on a Budget* and *Secrets for Great Sex After 50*.

JOAN DEFERS is a lover of manly men and fancy underpants. She blogs at JoanDefers.com, where she hopes to deliver quality erotic content to Internet smarties. She's currently working on a short-story collection, and she's probably just two innocent mistakes away from a much-deserved spanking.

KIKI DELOVELY (kikidelovely.wordpress.com) is a queer femme writer/performer whose work has appeared in various publications, including *Best Lesbian Erotica 2011* and *2012*, *Salacious* Magazine, *Take Me There: Transgender and Genderqueer Erotica* and *Say Please: Lesbian BDSM Erotica*.

As a naughty girl on a journey of self-discovery as an erotic writer, **TAMSIN FLOWERS** is as keen to entertain her readers as she is to explore every aspect of female erotica. She writes light-hearted stories that are perfect for reading on your own or with someone in whom you have more than a passing interest....

SACCHI GREEN's (sacchi-green.blogspot.com) stories have appeared in a hip-high stack of publications with erotically inspirational covers, and she's also edited eight erotica anthologies, including *Lipstick on Her Collar, Girl Crazy, Lesbian Cowboys* (winner of a Lambda Literary Award), *Lesbian Cops* and *Girl Fever*.

DAN GROGAN has lived most of his years in the open spaces and high plateaus of the western United States but has since been transplanted to Appalachia. He loves the music of that region and finds learning to play the banjo a sublime (and humbling) experience.

Writing by **TAHIRA IQBAL** (tahiraiqbal.com) can be found in numerous anthologies. Check out *Red Velvet and Absinthe*; *Cowboy Lust: Erotic Romance for Women*; *She-Shifters: Lesbian Paranormal Erotica* and *Suite Encounters: Hotel Sex Stories* for her work.

KRISTINA LLOYD (kristinalloyd.co.uk) is the author of four Black Lace novels including the erotic suspense-thrillers, *Asking for Trouble* and her latest book, *Thrill Seeker*. Her short stories have appeared in numerous anthologies, including several "best of" collections, and her work has been translated into German, Dutch and Japanese.

SOMMER MARSDEN's (sommermarsden.blogspot.com) short work has appeared in over one hundred print anthologies. And she's not done yet. Sommer is the author of *Restless Spirit, Big Bad* and numerous other erotic novels.

DEREK MCDANIEL's writing has previously appeared in the anthologies *Hot Spots: Erotic Tales of Computer Sex and Online Domination* and *On Display: Tales of Male Dominants and Female Exhibitionists*. He lives in California with, at present, a girlfriend, a slave, and a husky.

MOLLY MOORE is the writer of one of the United Kingdom's most successful sex blogs, Molly's Daily Kiss. Her blog is a marriage of words and images and most of her writing is based on her own experiences and contains strong autobiographical content. She lives a 24/7 D/s based relationship as a submissive woman.

N. T. MORLEY (ntmorley.com) is the author of twenty-four published novels and the editor of the best-selling anthology *Master/slave*. Morley's recent books include *Doctor's Orders: Stories of Extreme Medical Play* and *Double Vision: Erotic Tales of Bi Men Who Share*.

MEADOW PARKER is the pseudonym of a semi-secretly kinky Oakland, California tech writer who remains happily single and provocatively available, at least until the right semi-famous toppy couple comes along to claim her.

SADEY QUINN (sadeyquinn.com) is an erotic fiction writer living in Austin, Texas. Her works include novels *Under Order* and *Social Service* and novellas *Under His Roof* and *Under His Hand*. When Ms. Quinn isn't writing, she spends time cooking up delicious food and drinking red wine with good friends.

GISELLE RENARDE is a queer Canadian, avid volunteer, contributor to more than fifty short-story anthologies and author of dozens of electronic and print books, including *Anonymous, Ondine* and *My Mistress' Thighs*.

TERESA NOELLE ROBERTS writes romantic erotica and erotic romance for lusty romantics of all persuasions. Her work has appeared in *The Big Book of Bondage*; *Best Bondage Erotica 2011, 2012* and *2013; Orgasmic*; *Playing with Fire* and other anthologies with provocative titles. She writes erotic romance for Samhain and Phaze.

THOMAS S. ROCHE's (thomasroche.com) novel *The Panama Laugh* was a finalist for the Bram Stoker Award from the Horror Writers' Association. He is the author of several hundred published short stories and the coauthor, with Alison Tyler, of *His* and *Hers*.

AUBURN SANDERS's erotic bondage, SM and D/s fiction has appeared in the anthologies *Bitter Sweets, Hot Pink* and *You Belong to Me*.

J. SINCLAIRE (lusting.ca) is a Toronto-based writer by profession but erotic by nature. Her work has appeared in anthologies such as *Cheeky Spanking Stories, Lips Like Sugar* and *The Happy Birthday Book of Erotica*.

SOPHIA VALENTI (sophiavalenti.blogspot.com) is the author of *Indecent Desires*, an erotic novella of spanking and submission. Her fiction has appeared in the Harlequin Spice anthologies *Alison's Wonderland* and *With This Ring, I Thee Bed*, as well as several Pretty Things Press books, including *Kiss My Ass, Skirting the Issue, Bad Ass* and *Torn*.

VERONICA WILDE (veronicawilde.com) is an erotic romance author whose work has been published by Cleis Press, Bella Books, Xcite Books, Liquid Silver Books and Samhain Publishing.

ABOUT
THE EDITOR

Called "a trollop with a laptop" by *East Bay Express,* "a literary siren" by Good Vibrations and "the mistress of literary erotica" by Violet Blue, **ALISON TYLER** is naughty and she knows it. Over the past two decades, Ms. Tyler has written more than twenty-five explicit novels, including *Tiffany Twisted, Melt with You* and *The ESP Affair.* Her novels and short stories have been translated into Japanese, Dutch, German, Italian, Norwegian, Spanish and Greek. When not writing sultry short stories, she edits erotic anthologies, including *Alison's Wonderland, Kiss My Ass, Skirting the Issue* and *Torn.* She is also the author of several novellas including *Cuffing Kate, Giving In* and *A Taste of Chi.*

Ms. Tyler is loyal to coffee (black), lipstick (red), and tequila (straight). She has tattoos, but no piercings; a wicked tongue, but a quick smile; and bittersweet memories, but no regrets. She believes it won't rain if she doesn't bring an umbrella, prefers hot and dry to cold and wet, and loves to spout her favorite motto:

You can sleep when you're dead. She chooses Led Zeppelin over the Beatles, the Cure over NIN, and the Stones over everyone. Although she appreciates good rock, she has a pitiful weakness for '80s hair bands.

In all things important, she remains faithful to her partner of seventeen years, but she still can't choose just one perfume.

More from Alison Tyler

Frenzy
60 Stories of Sudden Sex
Edited by Alison Tyler

"Toss out the roses and box of candies. This isn't a prolonged seduction. This is slammed against the wall in an alleyway sex, and it's all that much hotter for it."
—Erotica Readers & Writers Association
ISBN 978-1-57344-331-9 $14.95

Best Bondage Erotica
Edited by Alison Tyler

Always playful and dangerously explicit, these arresting fantasies grab you, tie you down, and never let you go.
ISBN 978-1-57344-173-5 $15.95

Afternoon Delight
Erotica for Couples
Edited by Alison Tyler

"Alison Tyler evokes a world of heady sensuality where fantasies are fearlessly explored and dreams gloriously realized."
—Barbara Pizio, Executive Editor,
Penthouse Variations
ISBN 978-1-57344-341-8 $14.95

Got a Minute?
60 Second Erotica
Edited by Alison Tyler

"Classy but very, very dirty, this is one of the few very truly indispensable filth anthologies around." —*UK Forum*
ISBN 978-1-57344-404-0 $14.95

Playing with Fire
Taboo Erotica
Edited by Alison Tyler

"Alison Tyler has managed to find the best stories from the best authors, and create a book of fantasies that—if you're lucky enough, or determined enough—just might come true." —Clean Sheets
ISBN 978-1-57344-348-7 $14.95

Happy Endings Forever And Ever

Dark Secret Love
A Story of Submission
By Alison Tyler

Inspired by her own BDSM exploits and private diaries, Alison Tyler draws on twenty-five years of penning sultry stories to create a scorchingly hot work of fiction, a memoir-inspired novel with reality at its core. A modern-day *Story of O*, a *9 1/2 Weeks*-style journey fueled by lust, longing and the search for true love.
ISBN 978-1-57344-956-4 $16.95

High-Octane Heroes
Erotic Romance for Women
Edited by Delilah Devlin

One glance and your heart will melt—these chiseled, brave men will ignite your fantasies with their courage and charisma. Award-winning romance writer Delilah Devlin has gathered stories of hunky, red-blooded guys who enter danger zones in the name of duty, honor, country and even love.
ISBN 978-1-57344-969-4 $15.95

Duty and Desire
Military Erotic Romance
Edited by Kristina Wright

The only thing stronger than the call of duty is the call of desire. *Duty and Desire* enlists a team of hot-blooded men and women from every branch of the military who serve their country and follow their hearts.
ISBN 978-1-57344-823-9 $15.95

Smokin' Hot Firemen
Erotic Romance Stories for Women
Edited by Delilah Devlin

Delilah delivers tales of these courageous men breaking down doors to steal readers' hearts! *Smokin' Hot Firemen* imagines the romantic possibilities of being held against a massively muscled chest by a man whose mission is to save lives and serve *every* need.
ISBN 978-1-57344-934-2 $15.95

Only You
Erotic Romance for Women
Edited by Rachel Kramer Bussel

Only You is full of tenderness, raw passion, love, longing and the many emotions that kindle true romance. The couples in *Only You* test the boundaries of their love to make their relationships stronger.
ISBN 978-1-57344-909-0 $15.95

Many More Than Fifty Shades of Erotica

Please, Sir
Erotic Stories of Female Submission
Edited by Rachel Kramer Bussel

If you liked *Fifty Shades of Grey,* you'll love the explosive stories of *Please, Sir.* These damsels delight in the pleasures of taking risks to be rewarded by the men who know their deepest desires. Find out why nothing is as hot as the power of the words "Please, Sir."
ISBN 978-1-57344-389-0 $14.95

Yes, Sir
Erotic Stories of Female Submission
Edited by Rachel Kramer Bussel

Bound, gagged or spanked—or controlled with just a glance—these lucky women experience the breathtaking thrills of sexual submission. *Yes, Sir* shows that pleasure is best when dispensed by a firm hand.
ISBN 978-1-57344-310-4 $15.95

He's on Top
Erotic Stories of Male Dominance and Female Submission
Edited by Rachel Kramer Bussel

As true tops, the bossy hunks in these stories understand that BDSM is about exulting in power that is freely yielded. These kinky stories celebrate women who know exactly what they want.
ISBN 978-1-57344-270-1 $14.95

Best Bondage Erotica 2013
Edited by Rachel Kramer Bussel

Let *Best Bondage Erotica 2013* be your kinky playbook to erotic restraint—from silk ties and rope to shiny cuffs, blindfolds and so much more. These stories of forbidden desire will captivate, shock and arouse you.
ISBN 978-1-57344-897-0 $15.95

Luscious
Stories of Anal Eroticism
Edited by Alison Tyler

Discover all the erotic possibilities that exist between the sheets and between the cheeks in this daring collection. "Alison Tyler is an author to rely on for steamy, sexy page turners! Try her!"—Powell's Books
ISBN 978-1-57344-760-7 $15.95

Unleash Your Favorite Fantasies

The Big Book of Bondage
Sexy Tales of Erotic Restraint
Edited by Alison Tyler

Nobody likes bondage more than editrix Alison Tyler, who is
fascinated with the ecstasies of giving up, giving in, and en-
trusting one's pleasure (and pain) into the hands of another.
Delve into a world of unrestrained passion, where heart-stop-
ping dynamics will thrill and inspire you.
ISBN 978-1-57344-907-6 $15.95

Hurts So Good
Unrestrained Erotica
Edited by Alison Tyler

Intricately secured by ropes, locked in
handcuffs or bound simply by a lover's
command, the characters of *Hurts So Good*
find themselves in the throes of pleasurable
restraint in this indispensible collection by
prolific, award-winning editor Alison Tyler.
ISBN 978-1-57344-723-2 $14.95

Caught Looking
*Erotic Tales of Voyeurs and
Exhibitionists*
Edited by Alison Tyler
and Rachel Kramer Bussel

These scintillating fantasies take the reader
inside a world where people get to show
off, watch, and feel the vicarious thrill of
sex times two, their erotic power multiplied
by the eyes of another.
ISBN 978-1-57344-256-5 $14.95

Hide and Seek
*Erotic Tales of Voyeurs and
Exhibitionists*
Edited by Rachel Kramer Bussel
and Alison Tyler

Whether putting on a deliberate show
for an eager audience or peeking into the
hidden sex lives of their neighbors, these
show-offs and shy types go all out in their
quest for the perfect peep show.
ISBN 978-1-57344-419-4 $14.95

One Night Only
Erotic Encounters
Edited by Violet Blue

"Passion and lust play by different rules in
One Night Only. These are stories about
what happens when we have just that one
opportunity to ask for what we want—and
we take it... Enjoy the adventure."
—Violet Blue
ISBN 978-1-57344-756-0 $14.95

Red Hot Erotic Romance

**Buy 4 books,
Get 1 *FREE***

Best Erotica Series

"Gets racier every year."—San Francisco Bay Guardian

**Buy 4 books,
Get 1 FREE***

Best Women's Erotica 2013
Edited by Violet Blue
ISBN 978-1-57344-898-7 $15.95

Best Women's Erotica 2012
Edited by Violet Blue
ISBN 978-1-57344-755-3 $15.95

Best Women's Erotica 2011
Edited by Violet Blue
ISBN 978-1-57344-423-1 $15.95

Best Bondage Erotica 2013
Edited by Rachel Kramer Bussel
ISBN 978-1-57344-897-0 $15.95

Best Bondage Erotica 2012
Edited by Rachel Kramer Bussel
ISBN 978-1-57344-754-6 $15.95

Best Bondage Erotica 2011
Edited by Rachel Kramer Bussel
ISBN 978-1-57344-426-2 $15.95

Best Lesbian Erotica 2013
Edited by Kathleen Warnock.
Selected and introduced by
Jewelle Gomez.
ISBN 978-1-57344-896-3 $15.95

Best Lesbian Erotica 2012
Edited by Kathleen Warnock.
Selected and introduced by
Sinclair Sexsmith.
ISBN 978-1-57344-752-2 $15.95

Best Lesbian Erotica 2011
Edited by Kathleen Warnock.
Selected and introduced by Lea DeLaria.
ISBN 978-1-57344-425-5 $15.95

Best Gay Erotica 2013
Edited by Richard Labonté.
Selected and introduced by Paul Russell.
ISBN 978-1-57344-895-6 $15.95

Best Gay Erotica 2012
Edited by Richard Labonté.
Selected and introduced by
Larry Duplechan.
ISBN 978-1-57344-753-9 $15.95

Best Gay Erotica 2011
Edited by Richard Labonté.
Selected and introduced by
Kevin Killian.
ISBN 978-1-57344-424-8 $15.95

Best Fetish Erotica
Edited by Cara Bruce
ISBN 978-1-57344-355-5 $15.95

Best Bisexual Women's Erotica
Edited by Cara Bruce
ISBN 978-1-57344-320-3 $15.95

Best Lesbian Bondage Erotica
Edited by Tristan Taormino
ISBN 978-1-57344-287-9 $16.95

★ Free book of equal or lesser value. Shipping and applicable sales tax extra.
Cleis Press • (800) 780-2279 • orders@cleispress.com
www.cleispress.com

Out of This World Romance

Steamlust
Steampunk Erotic Romance
Edited by Kristina Wright

Shiny brass and crushed velvet; mechanical inventions and romantic conventions; sexual fantasy and kinky fetish: this is a
lush and fantastical world of women-centered stories and romantic scenarios, a first for steampunk fiction.
ISBN 978-1-57344-721-8 $14.95

The Sweetest Kiss
Ravishing Vampire Erotica
Edited by D. L. King

These sanguine tales give new meaning to
the term "dead sexy" and feature beautiful
bloodsuckers whose desires go far beyond
blood.
ISBN 978-1-57344-371-5 $15.95

Dream Lover
Paranormal Tales of Erotic Romance
Edited by Kristina Wright

A potent potion of fun and sexy tales
filled with male fairies and clairvoyant
scientists, as well as darkly erotic tales of
ghosts, shapeshifters and possession.
ISBN 978-1-57344-655-6 $14.95

Fairy Tale Lust
Erotic Fantasies for Women
Edited by Kristina Wright

Award-winning novelist and erotica
writer Kristina Wright goes over the
river and through the woods to find the
sexiest fairy tales ever written.
ISBN 978-1-57344-397-5 $14.95

In Sleeping Beauty's Bed
Erotic Fairy Tales
By Mitzi Szereto

"Who can resist the erotic origins of fairy
tales from Little Red to Rapunzel's long
braid? Szereto knows her way around the
mythic scholarship and the most outra-
geous sexual deviations in Pandora's Box."
                                    —Susie Bright
ISBN 978-1-57344-367-8 $16.95

Ordering is easy! Call us toll free or fax us to place your MC/VISA order.
You can also mail the order form below with payment to:
Cleis Press, 2246 Sixth St., Berkeley, CA 94710.

ORDER FORM

QTY	TITLE	PRICE

SUBTOTAL _____

SHIPPING _____

SALES TAX _____

TOTAL _____

Add $3.95 postage/handling for the first book ordered and $1.00 for each additional book. Outside North America, please contact us for shipping rates. California residents add 9% sales tax. Payment in U.S. dollars only.

* Free book of equal or lesser value. Shipping and applicable sales tax extra.

Cleis Press • Phone: (800) 780-2279 • Fax: (510) 845-8001
orders@cleispress.com • www.cleispress.com
You'll find more great books on our website

Follow us on Twitter @cleispress • Friend/fan us on Facebook